James Baird Mcclure

Wit, Wisdom, Eloquence, and Great Speeches of Col. R. G. Ingersoll

Including eloquent extracts, witty, wise, pungent, truthful sayings and full reports

of the great speeches of this celebrated man

James Baird Mcclure

Wit, Wisdom, Eloquence, and Great Speeches of Col. R. G. Ingersoll
Including eloquent extracts, witty, wise, pungent, truthful sayings and full reports of the great speeches of this celebrated man

ISBN/EAN: 9783337105389

Printed in Europe, USA, Canada, Australia, Japan

Cover: Foto ©Raphael Reischuk / pixelio.de

More available books at **www.hansebooks.com**

WIT,

WISDOM, ELOQUENCE,

AND

GREAT SPEECHES

OF

COL. R. G. INGERSOLL,

INCLUDING ELOQUENT EXTRACTS, WITTY, WISE, PUNGENT, TRUTH-
FUL SAYINGS AND FULL REPORTS OF THE GREAT SPEECHES
OF THIS CELEBRATED MAN, TOGETHER WITH THE
FUNERAL ORATION AT HIS BROTHER'S GRAVE.

EDITED BY

J. B. McCLURE.

CHICAGO:
RHODES & McCLURE, PUBLISHERS.
1881.

PREFACE.

The general public are quite familiar with the wit, wisdom, and eloquence of Col. R. G. Ingersoll. He certainly ranks among the first of living orators, and many of his sayings are as remarkable for terseness, pungency, and truthfulness, as can be found, perhaps, in the English tongue. The Compiler presents in this volume what he has selected with great care, and what he believes to be the wittiest, wisest and most eloquent words of this noted man.

The reader will also find a number of the Colonel's most eloquent and celebrated speeches given in full, including the remarkable funeral oration at his brother's grave.

J. B. McCLURE.

Chicago, June 20, 1881.

CONTENTS.

CONTENTS.

F.

8 *CONTENTS.*

INGERSOLL'S
WIT, WISDOM, ELOQUENCE,
AND
GREAT SPEECHES.

Human Happiness.

I tell you I had rather make somebody happy; I would
rather have the love of somebody; I would rather go to
the forest, far away, and build me a little cabin—bu'ld it
myself and daub it with mud, and live there with my wife

CABIN HOME OF LINCOLN'S PARENTS.

and children; I had rather go there and live by myself—
our little family—and have a little path that led down to
the spring, where the water bubbled out day and night like
a little poem from the heart of the earth; a little hut with
some hollyhocks at the corner, with their bannered bosoms

open to the sun, and with the thrush in the air, like a song
of joy in the morning; I would rather live there and have
some lattice work across the window, so that the sunlight
would fall checkered on the baby in the cradle; I would
rather live there and have my soul erect and free, than to
live in a palace of gold and wear the crown of imperial
power and know that my soul was slimy with hypocrisy.

It is not necessary to be rich and great and powerful in
order to be happy. If you will treat your wife like a
splendid flower, she will fill your life with a perfume and
with joy. I believe in the democracy of the fireside; I
believe in the republicanism of home; in the equality of
man and woman; in the equality of husband and wife.

Love vs. Glory.

A little while ago I stood by the grave of the old Napoleon—a magnificent tomb of gilt and gold, fit almost for a
dead deity—and gazed upon the sarcophagus of black Egyp-
tian marble, where rest at last the ashes of the restless man.
I leaned over the balustrade and thought about the career
of the greatest soldier of the modern world. I saw him
walking upon the banks of the Seine, contemplating suicide
—I saw him at Toulon—I saw him putting down the mob
in the streets of Paris—I saw him at the head of the army
of Italy—I saw him crossing the bridge of Lodi with the
tri-color in his hand—I saw him in Egypt in the shadows
of the pyramids—I saw him conquer the Alps and mingle
the eagles of France with the eagles of the crags. I saw
him at Marengo—at Ulm and Austerlitz. I saw him in
Russia, where the infantry of the snow and the cavalry of
the wild blast scattered his legions like Winter's withered
leaves. I saw him at Leipsic in defeat and disaster—driven

by a million bayonets back upon Paris—clutched like a wild
beast—banished to Elba. I saw him escape and retake an
empire by the force of his genius. I saw him upon the
frightful field of Waterloo, where chance and fate combined
to wreck the fortunes of their former king. And I saw him
at St. Helena, with his hands crossed behind him, gazing
out upon the sad and solemn sea. I thought of the orphans
and widows he had made—of the tears that had been shed
for his glory, and of the only woman who ever loved him,
pushed from his heart by the cold hand of ambition. And
I said I would rather have been a French peasant, and
worn wooden shoes. I would rather have lived in a hut
with a vine growing over the door, and the grapes growing
purple in the kisses of the Autumn sun. I would rather
have been that poor peasant with my loving wife by my
side, knitting as the day died out of the sky—with my
children upon my knees and their arms about me; I would
rather have been that man and gone down to the tongueless
silence of the dreamless dust, than to have been that imperial impersonation of force and murder known as Napoleon the Great. And so I would, ten thousand thousand
times.

Influence of a Home.

There can be no such thing in the highest sense as a
home, unless you own it. There must be an incentive to
plant trees, to beautify the grounds, to preserve and improve. It elevates a man to own a home. It gives a certain independence, a force of character that is obtained in
no other way. A man without a home feels like a passenger. There is in such a man a little of the vagrant. Homes
make patriots. He who has sat by his own fireside with

wife and children, will defend it. When he hears the word country pronounced, he thinks of his home.

Few men have been patriotic enough to shoulder a musket in defense of a boarding-house.

The prosperity and glory of our country depend upon the number of our people who are the owners of homes. Around the fireside cluster the private and the public virtues of our race. Raise your sons to be independent through labor—to pursue some business for themselves, and upon their own account—to be self-reliant—to act upon their own responsibility, and to take the consequences like men. Teach them above all things to be good, true and faithful husbands—winners of love, and builders of homes.

Ingersoll on Alcohol—A Scathing Denunciation.

Colonel Ingersoll, in speaking to a jury in a case which involved the manufacture of alcohol, used the following eloquent language:

"I am aware that there is a prejudice against any man engaged in the manufacture of alcohol. I believe that from the time it issues from the coiled and poisonous worm in the distillery until it empties into the hell of death, dishonor and crime, that it demoralizes everybody that touches it, from its source to where it ends. I do not believe anybody can contemplate the subject without becoming prejudiced against that liquor crime.

"All we have to do, gentlemen, is to think of the wrecks on either bank of the stream of death; of the suicides, of the insanity; of the poverty, of the ignorance, of the destitution; of the little children tugging at the faded and weary breasts of weeping and despairing wives, asking for bread; of the talented men of genius it has wrecked, the men struggling with imaginary serpents, produced by this devilish thing; and when you think of the jails, the alms-houses, of the asylums, of the prisons, of the scaffolds upon either bank, I do not wonder that every thoughtful man is prejudiced against this stuff called alcohol.

"Intemperance cuts down youth in its vigor, manhood in its strength, and age in its weakness. It breaks the father's heart, bereaves the doting mother, extinguishes natural affections, erases conjugal loves, blots out filial at-tachments, blights parental hope, and brings down mourn-ing age in sorrow to the grave. It produces weakness, not strength; sickness, not health; death, not life. It makes wives widows; children orphans; fathers fiends, and all of them paupers and beggars. It feeds rheumatism, nurses gout, welcomes epidemics, invites cholera, imports pestilence and embraces consumption. It covers the land with idleness, misery and crime. It fills your jails, supplies your alms-houses and demands your asylums. It engenders controversies, fosters quarrels, and cherishes riots. It crowds your penitentiaries and furnishes victims to your scaffolds. It is the life blood of the gambler, the element of the burglar, the prop of the highwayman and the support of the midnight incendiary. It countenances the liar, respects the thief, esteems the blasphemer. It violates obligations, reverences fraud, and honors infamy. It defames benevolence, hates love, scorns virtue and slanders innocence. It incites the father to butcher his helpless offspring, helps the husband to massacre his wife, and the child to grind the paricidal axe. It burns up men, consumes women, detests life, curses God, and despises heaven. It suborns witnesses, nurses perjury, defiles the jury box, and stains the judicial ermine. It degrades the citizen, debases the legislator, dishonors statesmen, and disarms the patriot. It brings shame, not honor; terror, not safety; despair, not hope; misery, not happiness; and with the malevolence of a fiend, it calmly surveys its frightful desolation, and unsatisfied with its havoc, it poisons felicity, kills peace, ruins morals, blights confidence, slays reputation, and wipes out national honors, then curses the world and laughs at its ruin.

"It does all that and more—it murders the soul. It is the son of villainies, the father of all crimes, the mother of abominations, the devil's best friend and God's worst enemy."

Ingersoll's "Honor Brights"—Love and Life.

—Without the family relation is tender, pure and true, civilization is impossible.

—I believe in marriage. If there is any Heaven upon earth, it is in the family by the fireside.

—The happy man is the successful man; and the man who makes somebody else happy, is a happy man.

—I believe marriage should be a perfect and equal partnership. I do not like a man who thinks he is boss.

—If there is a man I detest, it is the man who thinks he is the head of the family—the man who thinks he is "boss."

—I tell you this is a pretty good world, if we only love somebody in it; if we only make somebody happy; if we are only honor bright in it.

—I believe in marriage, and I hold in utter contempt the

opinions of long-haired men and short-haired women who denounce the institution of marriage.

—I do not like a man who thinks he has got authority, and that the woman belongs to him—that wants for his wife a slave. I would not have a slave for my wife.

—Love is the only thing that will pay ten per cent. of interest on the outlay. Love is the only thing in which the height of extravagance is the last degree of economy.

—The man who has the love of one splendid woman is a rich man. Joy is wealth, and love is the legal tender of the soul! Love is the only thing that will pay ten per cent. to borrower and lender both.

—I tell you it is an infamous word and an infamous feeling —a man who is "boss," who is going to govern in his family; and when he speaks let all the rest of them be still; some mighty idea is about to be launched from his mouth. Do you know I dislike this man?

--The man that has gained the love of one good, splendid, pure woman, his life has been a success, no matter if he dies in the ditch; and if he gets to be a crowned monarch of the world, and never had the love of one splendid heart, his life has been an ashen vapor.

—Now, my friends, it seems to me that the woman is the equal of the man. She has all the rights I have, and one more, and that is the right to be protected. That's my doctrine. You are married; try and make the woman you love happy; try and make the man you love happy.

—If you are the grand emperor of the world, you had better be the grand emperor of one loving and tender heart, and she the grand empress of yours. The man who has really won the love of one good woman in this world, I do not care if he dies a beggar, his life has been a success

—Imagine a young man and a young woman courting, walking out in the moonlight and the nightingale singing a song of pain and love, as though the thorn touched her heart—imagine them stopping there in the moonlight and starlight and song, and saying, "Now, here, let's settle who's 'boss!'"

—I have known men that would trust a woman with their heart (if you call that thing which pushes their blood around, a heart), and with their honor (if you call that fear of getting into the penitentiary, honor); I have known men that would trust that heart and that honor with a woman, but not their pocket-book—not a dollar bill.

—I have not the slightest respect for the ideas of those short-haired women and long-haired men who denounce the institution of the family; who denounce the institution of marriage; but I hold in greater contempt the husband who would enslave his wife. I hold in greater contempt the man who is anythir in his family except love and tenderness and kindness.

—What is wealth compared with the love of a splendid woman? People tell me that it is very good doctrine for rich folks, but it won't do for poor folks. I tell you that there is more love in the huts and homes of the poor, than in the mansions of the rich ; and the meanest hut with love in it is a palace fit for the gods, and a palace without that is a den only fit for wild beasts.

—Let me say right here, I regard marriage as the holiest institution among men. Without the fireside there is no human advancement; without the family relation there is no life worth living. Every good government is made up of good families. The unit of government is the family, and anything that tends to destroy the family is perfectly devilish and infamous.

—Whoever marries simply for himself will make a mistake; but whoever loves a woman so well that he says, "I
will make her happy," makes no mistake; and so with the
woman who says, "I will make him happy.". There is
only one way to be happy. and that is to make somebody
else so, and you can't be happy cross-lots; you have got to
go the regular turnpike road.

—I say it took hundreds of years for woman to come
from a state of slavery to marriage; and, ladies, the chains
that were upon your necks and the bracelets that were put
upon your arms were iron, and they have been changed by
the touch of the wand of civilization, to shining, glittering
gold. Woman came from a condition of abject slavery,
and thousands and thousands are in that condition now.

—Let me say right here—and I have thought a good
deal about it—let me say right here, the grandest ambition
that any man can possibly have, is to so live and so improve himself in heart and brain as to be worthy of the
love of some splendid woman; and the grandest ambition
of any girl is to make herself worthy of the love and ado-
ration of some magnificent man. That is my idea, and
there is no success in life without it.

—I would not want the love of a woman that is not great
enough, grand enough, and splendid enough to be free.
I will never give to any woman my heart upon whom I
afterwards would put chains. Do you know sometimes
I think generosity is about the only virtue there is? How
I do hate a man that has to be begged and importuned
every minute for a few cents by his wife. "Give me a
dollar?" "What did you do with that fifty cents I gave
you last Christmas?"

—When a man comes home let him come home like a
ray of light in the night bursting through the doors and

illuminating the darkness. What right has a man to assassinate joy, and murder happiness in the sanctuary of love —to be a cross man, a peevish man? Is that the way he courted? Was there always something ailing him? Was he too nervous to hear her speak? When I see a man of that kind I am always sorry that doctors know so much about preserving life as they do.

—I tell you women are more prudent than men. I tell you, as a rule, women are more truthful than men. I tell you that women are more faithful than men—ten times as faithful as man. I never saw a man pursue his wife into the very ditch and dust of degradation and take her in his arms. I never saw a man stand at the shore where she had been morally wrecked, waiting for the waves to bring back even her corpse to his arms; but I have seen woman do it. I have seen woman with her white arms lift man from the mire of degradation, and hold him to her bosom as though he were an angel.

—It is not necessary to be rich in order to be happy. It is only necessary to be in love. Thousands of men go to college and get a certificate that they have an education, and that certificate is in Latin, and they stop studying, and in two years to save their life they couldn't read the certificate they got. It is mostly so in marrying. They stop courting when they get married. They think, we have won her and that is enough. Ah! the difference before and after! How well they look! How bright their eyes! How light their steps, and how full they were of generosity and laughter! I tell you a man should consider himself in good luck if a woman loves him when he is doing his level best! Good luck! Good luck! And another thing that is the cause of much trouble is that people don't count fairly. They do what they call putting their best foot for-

ward. That means lying a little. I say put your worst
foot forward. If you have got any faults, admit them. If
you drink, say so and quit it. If you chew and smoke and
swear, say so. If some of your kindred are not very good
people, say so. If you have had two or three that died on
the gallows, or that ought to have died there, say so. Tell
all your faults, and if after she knows your faults she says
she will have you, you have got the dead wood on that
woman forever. I claim that there should be perfect

BIRTHPLACE OF GENERAL GRANT.

equality in the home, and I cannot think of anything nearer
Heaven than a home where there is true republicanism and
true democracy at the fireside. All are equal. And then,
do you know, I like to think that love is eternal; that if
you really love the woman, for her sake, you will love her
no matter what she may do; that if she really loves you,
for your sake, the same—if you really love her you will
always see the face you loved and won.

How They Did when Ingersoll was a Farmer.

When I was a farmer they used to haul wheat two hundred miles in a wagon and sell it for thirty-five cents a bushel. They would bring home about three hundred feet of lumber, two bunches of shingles, a barre. of salt, and a cook stove that never would draw and ever did bake.

In those blessed days the peo[,] lived on corn and bacon. Cooking was an unknown a . Eating was a necessity, not a pleasure. It was hard work for the cook to keep on good terms even with hunger.

The rain held the roofs in perfect contempt, and the snow drifted joyfully on the floors and beds. They had no barns. The horses were kept in rail pens surrounded with straw. Long before spring the sides would be eaten away and nothing but roofs would be left. Food is fuel. When the cattle were exposed to all the blasts of winter, it took all the corn and oats that could be stuffed into them to prevent actual starvation.

In those times farmers thought the best place for the pig-pen was immediately in front of the house. There is nothing like sociability.

Women were supposed to know the art of making fires without fuel. The wood-pile consisted, as a general thing, of one log, upon which an axe or two had been worn out in vain. There was nothing to kindle a fire with. Pickets were pulled from the garden fence, clap boards taken from the house, and every stray plank was seized upon for kindling. Everything was done in the hardest way. Everything about the farm was disagreeable. Nothing was kept in order. Nothing was preserved. The wagons stood in the sun and rain, and the plows rusted in the fields. There was no leisure, no feeling that the work was done. It was all labor and weariness and vexation of spirit. The crops were destroyed by wandering herds, or they were put in too late, or too early, or they were blown down, or caught by the frost, or devoured by bugs, or stung by flies, or eaten by worms, or carried away by birds, or dug up by gophers, or washed away by floods, or dried up by the sun, or rotted in the stack, or heated in the crib, or they all run to vines, or tops, or straw, or cobs. And when in spite of all these accidents that lie in wait between the plow and the reaper, they did succeed in raising a good crop and a high price was offered, then the roads would be impassable. And when the roads got good, then the prices went down. Everything worked together for evil.

Nearly every farmer's boy took an oath that he would never cultivate the soil. The moment they arrived at the age of twenty-one they left the desolate and dreary farms and rushed to the towns and cities. They wanted to be book-keepers, doctors, merchants, railroad men, insurance agents, lawyers, even preachers, anything to avoid the drudgery of the farm. Nearly every boy acquainted with the three R's—reading, writing and arithmetic—imagined that he had altogether more education than ought to be wasted in raising potatoes and corn. They made haste to get into some other business. Those who stayed upon the farm envied those who went away.

A few years ago the times were prosperous, and the young men went to the cities to enjoy the fortunes that were waiting for them. They wanted to engage in something that promised quick returns. They built railways, established banks and insurance companies. They speculated in stocks in Wall street, and gambled in grain at Chicago. They became rich. They lived in palaces. They rode in carriages. They pitied their poor brothers on the farms, and the poor brothers envied them.

But time has brought its revenge. The farmers have seen

the railroad president a bankrupt, and the road in the hands of a receiver. They have seen the bank president abscond, and the insurance company a wrecked and ruined fraud. The only solvent people, as a class, the only independent people, are the tillers of the soil.

Liberty of Mind.

I do not know what inventions are in the brain of the future; I do not know what garments of glory may be woven for the world in the loom of years to be; we are just on the edge of the great ocean of discovery. I do not know what is to be discovered; I do not know what science will do for us. I do not know that science did just take a handful of sand and make the telescope, and with it read all the starry leaves of heaven; I know that science took the thunderbolts from the hands of Jupiter, and now the electric spark, freighted with thought and love, flashes under waves of the sea; I know that science stole a tear from the cheek of unpaid labor, converted it into steam, and created a giant that turns with tireless arms the countless wheels of toil; I know that science broke the chains from human limbs and gave us instead the forces of nature for our slaves; I know that we have made the attraction of gravitation work for us; we have made the lightnings our messengers; we have taken advantage of fire and flames and wind and sea; these slaves have no backs to be whipped; they have no hearts to be lacerated; they have no children to be stolen, no cradles to be violated. I know that science has given us better houses; I know it has given us better pictures and better books; I know it has given us better wives and better husbands, and more beautiful children. I know it has enriched a thousand-fold

our lives; and for that reason I am in favor of intellectual
liberty.

The Happy Farmer.

There is a quiet about the life of a farmer, and the hope
of a serene old age, that no other business or profession can
promise.   A professional man is doomed some time to feel
that his powers are waning.   He is doomed to see younger
and stronger men pass him in the race of life.   He looks
forward to an old age of intellectual mediocrity.   He will
be last where once he was the first.   But the farmer goes,
as it were, into partnership with nature—he lives with trees

and flowers—he breathes the sweet air of the fields. There is no constant and frightful strain upon his mind. His nights are filled with sleep and rest. He watches his flocks and herds as they feed upon the green and sunny slopes. He hears the pleasant rain falling upon the waving corn, and the trees he planted in youth rustle above him as he plants others for the children yet to be.

When I was a farmer it was not fashionable to set out trees, nor to plant vines.

When you visited the farm you were not welcomed by flowers, and greeted by trees loaded with fruit. Yellow dogs came bounding over the tumbled fence like wild beasts. There is no sense—there is no profit in such a life. It is not living. The farmers ought to beautify their homes. There should be trees and grass, and flowers and running vines. Everything should be kept in order ; gates should be kept on their hinges, and about all there should be the pleasant air of thrift. In every house there should be a bath-room. The bath is a civilizer, a refiner, a beautifier. When you come from the fields, tired, covered with dust, nothing is so refreshing. Above all things, keep clean. It is not necessary to be a pig in order to raise one. In the cool of the evening, after a day in the field, put on clean clothes, take a seat under the trees, 'mid the perfume of flowers, surrounded by your family, and you will know what it is to enjoy life like a gentleman.

The Kingdom of Kindness.

Above all, let every man treat his wife and children with infinite kindness. Give your sons and daughters every advantage within your power. In the air of kindness they will grow about you like flowers. They will fill your homes with sunshine and all your years with joy. Do not try to rule by force.

A blow from a parent leaves a scar on the soul. I should feel ashamed to die surrounded by children I had whipped. Think of feeling upon your dying lips the kiss of a child you had struck.

See to it that your wife has every convenience. Make her life worth living. Never allow her to become a servant. Wives, weary and worn; mothers, wrinkled and bent before their time, fill homes with grief and shame. If you are not able to hire help for your wives, help them yourselves. See that they have the best utensils to work with. Women cannot create things by magic. Have plenty of wood and coal—good cellars and plenty in them.

The Man that Ingersoll Hates.

A cross man I hate above all things. What right has ne to murder the sunshine of the day? What right has he to assassinate the joy of life? When you go home you ought to feel the light there is in the house; if it is in the night it will burst out of the doors and windows and illuminate the darkness. It is just as well to go home a ray of sunshine as an old, sour, cross curmudgeon, who thinks he is the head of the family. Wise men think their mighty brains have been in a turmoil; they have been thinking about who will be alderman from the fifth ward; they have been thinking about politics; great and mighty questions have been engaging their minds; they have bought calico at eight cents or six, and want to sell it for seven. Think of the intellectual strain that must have been upon a man, and when he gets home everybody else in the house must look out for his comfort. A woman who has only taken

care of five or six children, and one or two of them may be
sick, has been nursing them and singing to them, and taking
care of them, and trying to make one yard of cloth do the
work of two, she, of course, is fresh and fine and ready to
wait upon this great gentleman—the head of the family. I
don't like him a bit!

Industry,

We must get rid of the idea that a little learning unfits
one for work. There are hundreds of graduates of Yale
and Harvard and other colleges, who are agents of sewing
machines, solicitors for insurance, clerks, copyists, in short,
performing a hundred varieties of menial service. They
seem willing to do anything that is not regarded as work—
anything that can be done in a town, in the house, in an
office, but they avoid farming as they would leprosy.
Nearly every young man educated in this way is simply
ruined. Such an education ought to be called ignorance.
It is a thousand times better to have common sense without
education than education without the sense. Boys and girls
should be educated to help themselves. They should be
taught that it is disgraceful to be idle, and dishonorable to
be useless.

You can divide mankind into two classes; the laborers
and the idlers, the supporters and the supported, the honest
and the dishonest. Every man is dishonest who lives upon
the unpaid labor of others, no matter if he occupies a throne.
All laborers should be brothers. The laborers should have
equal rights before the world and before the law. And I
want every farmer to consider every man who labors either
with hand or brain as his brother. Until genius and labor
formed a partnership there was no such thing as prosperity
among men. Every reaper and mower, every agricultural

implement, has elevated work of the farmer, and his vocation grows grander with every invention.   In the olden
time the agriculturist was ignorant; he knew nothing of
machinery, he was the slave of superstition.

Ingersoll Believes in Fashion, Good Clothes, Etc.

I am a believer in fashion.   It is the duty of every
woman to make herself as beautiful and attractive as she
possibly can.

"Handsome is as handsome does," but she is much
handsomer if well dressed.   Every man should look his
very best.   I am a believer in good clothes.   The time
never ought to come in this country when you can tell a
farmer's daughter simply by the garments she wears.   I say
to every girl and woman, no matter what the material of
your dress may be, no matter how cheap and coarse it is,
cut it and make it in the fashion.   I believe in jewelry.
Some people look upon it as barbaric, but in my judgment,
wearing jewelry is the first evidence the barbarian gives of
a wish to be civilized.   To adorn ourselves seems to be a
part of our nature, and this desire seems to be everywhere
and in everything.   I have sometimes thought that the desire for beauty covers the earth with flowers.   It is this
desire that paints the wings of moths, tints the chamber of
the shell, and gives the bird its plumage and its song.   Oh!
daughters and wives if you would be loved, adorn yourselves—if you would be adored, be beautiful!

Civilizing Influence of Woman.

I don't believe man ever came to any high station without woman.   There has got to be some restraint, something
to make you prudent, something to make you industrious.

And in a country where you don't need any bed-quilt but
a cloud, revolution is the normal condition of the people.
You have got to have the fireside; you have got to have
the home, and there by the fireside will grow and bloom
the fruits of the human race. I recollect a while ago I was
in Washington when they were trying to annex Santo Domingo. They said: "We want to take in Santo Domingo."
Says I: "We don't want it." "Why," said they, "it is
the best climate the earth can produce. There is everything you want." "Yes," said I, "but it won't produce
men. We don't want it. We have got soil enough now.
Take 5,000 ministers from New England, 5,000 presidents
of colleges, and 5,000 solid business men and their families, and take them to Santo Domingo; and then you will
see the effect of climate. The second generation you will
see barefooted boys riding bareback on a mule, with their
hair sticking out of the top of their sombreros, with a
rooster under each arm going to a cock-fight on Sunday."
You have got to have the soil; you have got to have the
climate, and you have got to have another thing—you have
got to have the fireside.

Love and Joy.

It is not necessary to be great to be happy; it is not
necessary to be rich to be just and generous, and to have a
heart filled with divine affection. No matter whether you
are rich or poor, use your wife as though she were a splendid creation, and she will fill your life with perfume and
joy. And do you know it is a splendid thing for me to
think that the woman you really love will never grow old
to you. Through the wrinkles of time, through the music
of years, if you really love her, you will always see the

face you loved and won. And a woman who really loves a man, does not see that he grows older; he is not decrepit; he does not tremble; he is not old; she always sees the same gallant gentleman who won her hand and heart. I like to think of it in that way; I like to think of all passions; love is eternal, and as Shakspeare says, "Although time with his sickle can rob ruby lips and sparkling eyes, let him reach as far as he can, he cannot quite touch love, that reaches even to the end of the tomb." And to love in that way and then go down the hill of life together, and as you go down, hear, perhaps, the laughter of grandchildren, and the birds of joy and love will sing once more in the leafless branches of age. I believe in the fireside. I believe in the democracy of home. I believe in the republicanism of the family. I believe in liberty and equality with those we love.

A Short Patent Lecture.

I despise a stingy man. I don't see how it is possible for a man to die worth fifty millions of dollars or ten millions of dollars, in a city full of want, when he meets almost every day the withered hand of beggary and the white lips of famine. How a man can withstand all that, and hold in the clutch of his greed twenty or thirty millions of dollars, is past my comprehension. I do not see how he can do it. I should not think he could do it any more than he could keep a pile of lumber where hundreds and thousands of men were drowning in the sea. I should not think he could do it. Do you know I have known men who would trust their wives with their hearts and their honor, but not with their pocketbook; not with a dollar. When I see a man of that kind I always think he knows which of these articles is the most valuable.

Think of making your wife a beggar! Think of her having to ask you every day for a dollar, or for two dollars, or for fifty cents! "What did you do with that dollar I gave you last week?"

Think of having a wife that was afraid of you! What kind of children do you expect to have with a beggar and a coward for their mother? Oh! I tell you if you have but a dollar in the world and you have got to spend it, spend it like a king; spend it as though it were a dry leaf and you the owner of unbounded forests! That's the way to spend it!

I had rather be a beggar and spend my last dollar like a king, than be a king and spend my money like a beggar. If it's got to go, let it go. Get the best you can for your family—try to look as well as you can yourself.

When you used to go courting, how nice you looked! Ah, your eye was bright, your step was light, and you just put on the very best look you could. Do you know that it is insufferable egotism in you to suppose that a woman is going to love you always looking as bad as you can? Think of it! Any woman on earth will be true, to you forever when you do your level best. Some people tell me, "Your doctrine about loving and wives and all that is splendid for the rich, but it won't do for the poor." I tell you to-night there is on the average more love in the homes of the poor than in the palaces of the rich; and the meanest hut with love in it is fit for the gods, and a palace without love is a den only fit for wild beasts. That's my doctrine! You can't be so poor but that you can help somebody.

Good nature is the cheapest commodity in the world; and love is the only thing that will pay ten per cent. to borrower and lender both. Don't tell me that you have got to be rich! We have all a false standard of greatness in the United States. We think here that a man to be great must be notorious; he must be extremely wealthy or his name must be between the lips of rumor. It is all nonsense!

It is not necessary to be rich to be great, or to be power-ful to be happy; and the happy man is the successful man. Happiness is the legal-tender of the soul. Joy is wealth.

Illinois.

Let me tell you something about Illinois. We have fifty-six thousand square miles of land—nearly thirty-six million acres. Upon these plains we can raise enough to feed and clothe twenty million people. Beneath these prairies were hidden, millions of ages ago, by that old miser, the sun, thirty-six thousand square miles of coal. The aggregate thickness of these veins is at least fifteen feet. Think of a column of coal one mile square and one hundred miles high! All this came from the sun. What a sunbeam such a column would be! Think of all this force, willed and left to us by the dead morning of the world! Think of the fireside of the future around which will sit the fathers, mothers and children of the years to be! Think of the sweet and happy faces, the loving and tender eyes that will glow and gleam in the sacred light of all these flames!

Ingersollisms.

—Nothing is ever made by rascality.

—It is necessary to the happiness of man that he be faithful to himself.

—It will take thousands of years before the world will believingly say " Right makes might."

—It takes a great deal of trouble to raise a good Republican.

—A mortgage casts a shadow on the sunniest field. There is no business under the sun that can pay ten per cent.

—Every good man who has ever lived in the country, no matter whether he has been persecuted or not, has made the world better.

—I know enough to know that agriculture is the basis of all wealth, prosperity and luxury. I know that in the country where the tillers of the fields are free, everybody is free and ought to be prosperous.

—Free speech is the brain of the Republic; an honest ballot is the breath of its life, and honest money is the blood that courses through its veins.

—It is a splendid fact in nature that you cannot put chains upon the limbs of others without putting corresponding manacles upon your own brain.

—I propose to stand by the Nation. .I want the furnaces kept hot. I want the sky to be filled with the smoke of American industry, and upon that cloud of smoke will rest forever the bow of perpetual promise.

—The ballot box is the throne of America; the ballot box is the ark of the covenant. Unless we see to it that every man who has a right to vote votes, and unless we see to it that every honest vote is counted, the days of the Republic are numbered.

—Why is it that New England, a rock-clad land, blossoms like a rose? Why is it that New York is the Empire State of the great Union? I will tell you. Because you have been permitted to trade in ideas.

In every government there is something that ought to be preserved; in every government there are many things that ought to be destroyed. Every good man, every patriot, every lover of the human race, wishes to preserve the good and destroy the bad.

—I despise the doctrine of State sovereignty. I believe in the rights of the States, but not in the sovereignty of the States. States are political conveniences. Rising above States as the Alps above valleys are the rights of man. Rising above the rights of the government even in this Nation are the sublime rights of the people. Governments are good only so long as they protect human rights. But the rights of a man never should be sacrificed upon the altar of the State or upon the altar of the Nation.

—I am the sole proprietor of myself. No party, no organization, has any deed of trust on what little brains I have, and as long as I can get my part of the common air I am going to tell my honest thoughts. One man in the right will finally get to be a majority.

—Years ago I made up my mind that there was no particular argument in slander. I made up my mind that for parties as well as for individuals, honesty in the long run is the best policy. I made up my mind that the people were entitled to know a man's honest thoughts.

—I like a black man who loves this country better than I do a white man who hates it. I think more of a black man who fought for our flag than for any white man who endeavored to tear it out of heaven! I like black friends better than white enemies. And I think more of a man black outside and white inside than I do of one white outside and black inside.

—The old way of farming was a great mistake. Everything was done the wrong way. It was all work and waste, weariness and want. They used to fence a hundred and sixty acres of land with a couple of dogs. Everything was left to the blessed trinity of chance, accident and mistake.

—I am in favor of the idea of the great and splendid truth that this is a Nation one and indivisible. I deny that we are a confederacy bound together with ropes of cloud and chains of mist. This is a Nation, and every man in it owes his first allegiance to the grand old flag for which more blood was shed than for any other flag that waves in the sight of heaven.

—I am not only in favor of free speech, but I am also in favor of an absolutely honest ballot. There is one king in this country; there is one emperor; there is one supreme czar; and that is the legally expressed will of the majority of the people. The man who casts an illegal vote, the man who refuses to count a legal vote, poisons the fountain of power, poisons the spring of justice, and is a traitor to the only king in this land.

—I have always said; and I say again, that the more liberty there is given away, the more you have. There is room in this world for us all; there is room enough for all of our thoughts; out upon the intellectual sea there is room for every sail, and in the intellectual air there is space for every wing. A man that exercises a right that he will not give to others is a barbarian. A State that does not allow free speech is uncivilized, and is a disgrace to the American Union.

—I have been told that during the war we had plenty of money. I never saw it. I lived years without seeing a dollar. I saw promises for dollars, but not dollars. And the greenback, unless you have the gold behind it, is no more a dollar than a bill of fare is a dinner. You cannot make a paper dollar without taking a dollar's worth of paper. We must have paper that represents money. I want it issued by the government, and I want behind every one of these dollars either a gold or silver dollar, so that every greenback under the flag can lift up its hand and swear, "I know that my redeemer liveth."

Ingersoll's Eloquent Vision.

The following remarkably eloquent words are taken from Col. Ingersoll's brilliant address to the veteran soldiers at Indianapolis:

The past, as it were, rises before me like a dream. Again we are in the great struggle for National life. We hear the sound of preparation—the music of the boisterous drums—the silver voices of the heroic bugles. We see thousands of assemblages, and hear the appeals of orators; we see the pale cheeks of women, and the flushed faces of men; and in those assemblages we see all the dead whose dust we have covered with flowers. We lose sight of them no more. We are with them when they enlist in the great army of freedom. We see them part with those they love. Some are walking for the last time in quiet woody places with the maidens they adore. We hear the whisperings and the sweet vows of eternal love as they lingeringly part forever. Others are bending over cradles kissing babies that are asleep. Some are receiving the blessings of old men. Some are parting with mothers who hold them and press them to their hearts again and again, and say nothing; and some are talking with wives, and endeavoring with brave words spoken in the old tones to drive away the awful fear. We see them part. We see the wife standing in the door with the babe in her arms—standing in the sunlight sobbing—at the turn of the road a hand waves—she answers by holding high in her loving hands the child. He is gone, and forever.

We see them all as they march proudly away under the flaunting flags, keeping time to the wild grand music of war—marching down the streets of the great cities—through the towns and across the prairies—down to the fields of glory, to do and to die for the eternal right.

We go with them one and all. We are by their side on all the gory fields, in all the hospitals of pain—on all the weary marches. We stand guard with them in the wild storm and under the quiet stars. We are with them in ravines running with blood—in the furrows of old fields. We are with them between contending hosts, unable to move, wild with thirst, the life ebbing slowly away among the withered leaves. We see them pierced by balls and torn with shells in the trenches of forts, and in the whirlwind of the charge, where men become iron with nerves of steel.

We are with them in the prisons of hatred and famine, but human speech can never tell what they endured.

We are at home when the news comes that they are dead.

We see the maiden in the shadow of her sorrow. We see the silvered head of the old man bowed with the last grief. The past rises before us, and we see four millions of human beings governed by the lash—we see them bound hand and foot—we hear the strokes of cruel whips—we see hounds tracking women through tangled swamps. We see babes sold from the breasts of mothers. Cruelty unspeakable! Outrage infinite!

Four million bodies in chains—four million souls in fetters. All the sacred relations of wife, mother, father and child, trampled beneath the brutal feet of might. And all this was done under our own beautiful banner of the free.

The past rises before us. We hear the roar and shriek of the bursting shell. The broken fetters fall. There heroes died. We look. Instead of slaves we see men and women and children. The wand of progress touches the auction-block, the slave-pen, and the whipping-post and we see homes and firesides, and school-houses and books, and where all was want and crime, and cruelty and fear, we see the faces of the free.

These heroes are dead. They died for liberty—they died for us. They are at rest. They sleep in the land they made free, under the flag they rendered stainless, under the solemn pines, the sad hemlocks, the tearful willows, the embracing vines. They sleep beneath the shadows of the clouds, careless alike of sunshine or storm, each in the windowless palace of rest. Earth may run red with other wars—they are at peace. In the midst of battle, in the roar of conflict, they found the serenity of death. I have one sentiment for the soldiers living and dead—cheers for the living and tears for the dead.

The Colonel's Faith in American Labor.

I believe in American labor, and I tell you why. The other day a man told me that we had produced in the United States of America one million tons of rails. How much are they worth? Sixty dollars a ton. In other words, the million tons are worth $60,000,000. How much is a ton of iron worth in the ground? Twenty-five cents. American labor takes 25 cents of iron in the ground and adds to it $59.75. One million tons of rails, and the raw material not worth $24.000. We build a ship in the United States worth $500,000, and the value of the ore in the earth, of the trees in the great forest, of all that enters into the composition of that ship bringing $500,000 in gold is only $20,000; $480,C00 by American labor, American muscle, coined into gold; American brains made a legal-tender the world around.

The Independent Man.

It is a thousand times better to be a whole farmer than part of a mechanic. It is better to till the ground and work for yourself than to be hired by corporations. Every man should endeavor to belong to himself.

About seven hundred years ago, Kheyam, a Persian, said : "Why should a man who possesses a piece of bread securing life for two days, and who has a cup of water—why should such a man serve another?"

Young men should not be satisfied with a salary. Do not mortgage the possibilities of your future. Have the courage to take life as it comes, feast or famine. Think of hunting a gold mine for a dollar a day, and think of finding one for another man. How would you feel then?

We are lacking in true courage, when, for fear of the

future, we take the crusts and scraps and niggardly salaries of the present. I had a thousand times rather have a farm and be independent, than to be President of the United States, without independence, filled with doubt and trembling, feeling of the popular pulse, resorting to art and arttifice, inquiring about the wind of opinion, and succeeding at last in losing my self-respect without gaining the respect of others.

Man needs more manliness, more real independence. We must take care of ourselves. This we can do by labor, and in this way we can preserve our independence. We should try and choose that business or profession, the pursuit of which will give us the most happiness. Happiness is wealth. We can be happy without being rich—without holding office—without being famous. I am not sure that we can be happy with wealth, with office, or with fame.

What a Dollar Can Do.

Ainsworth R. Spofford—says Col. Ingersoll—gives the following facts about interest:

"One dollar loaned for one hundred years at six per cent., with the interest collected annually and added to the principal, will amount to three hundred and forty dollars. At eight per cent. it amounts to two thousand two hundred and three dollars. At three per cent. it amounts only to nineteen dollars and twenty-five cents. At ten per cent. it is thirteen thousand eight hundred and nine dollars, or about seven hundred times as much. At twelve per cent. it amounts to eighty-four thousand and seventy-five dollars, or more than four thousand times as much. At eighteen per cent. it amounts to fifteen million one hundred and forty-five thousand and seven dollars. At twenty-four per cent. (which we sometimes hear talked of) it reaches the enormous sum of two billion five hundred and fifty-one million seven hundred and ninety-five thousand four hundred and four dollars."

One dollar at compound interest, at twenty-four per cent., for one hundred years, would produce a sum equal to our national debt.

Interest eats night and day, and the more it eats the hungrier it grows. The farmer in debt, lying awake at night, can, if he listens, hear it gnaw. If he owes nothing, he can hear his corn grow. Get out of debt as soon as you possibly can. You have supported idle avarice and lazy economy long enough.

The Colonel's Party.

I wish to belong to that party which is prosperous when the country is prosperous. I belong to that party which is not poor when the golden billows are running over the seas of wheat. I belong to that party that is prosperous when there are oceans of corn, and when the cattle are upon the thousand hills. I belong to that party which is prosperous when the furnaces are aflame; and when you dig coal and iron and silver; when everybody has enough to eat; when everybody is happy; when the children are all going to school; and when joy covers my nation as with a garment. That party which is prosperous then, that is my party.

How the Colonel Cooks Beefsteak.

There ought to be a law making it a crime, punishable by imprisonment, to fry beefsteak. Broil it; it is just as easy, and when broiled it is delicious. Fried beefsteak is not fit for a wild beast. You can broil even on a stove.

Shut the front damper—open the back one, then take of a griddle. There will then be a draft down through this opening. Put on your steak, using a wire broiler, and not a particle of smoke will touch it, for the reason that the smoke goes down. If you try to broil it with the front damper open, the smoke will rise. For broiling, coal, even soft coal, makes a better fire than wood.

How Ingersoll Hopes to End His Days.

I can imagine no condition that carries with it such a promise of joy as that of the farmer in the early winter. He has his cellar filled—he has made every preparation for the days of snow and storm—he looks forward to three months of ease and rest; to three months of fireside content; three months with wife and children; three months of long, delightful evenings; three months of home; three months of solid comfort.

When the life of the farmer is such as I have described, the cities and towns will not be filled with want—the streets will not be crowded with wrecked rogues, broken bankers, and bankrupt speculators. The fields will be tilled, and country villages, almost hidden by trees, and vines, and flowers, filled with industrious and happy people, will nestle in every vale and gleam like gems on every plain.

The idea must be done away with that there is something intellectually degrading in cultivating the soil. Nothing can be nobler than to be useful. Idleness should not be respectable.

If farmers will cultivate well, and without waste; if they will so build that their houses will be warm in winter and cool in summer; if they will plant trees and beautify their homes; if they will occupy their leisure in reading, in thinking, in improving their minds and in devising ways

and means to make their business profitable and pleasant ;
if they will live nearer together and cultivate sociability ;
if they will come together often; if they will have reading
rooms and cultivate music; if they wil have bath-rooms,
ice-houses and good gardens; if their wives can have an
easy time ; if the nights can be taken for sleep and the ev-
-enings for enjoyment, everybody will be in love with the
fields.   Happiness should be the object of life, and if life
on the farm can be ma le really happy, the children will
grow up in love with the meadows, the streams, the woods
and the old home.   Around the farm will cling and cluster
the happy memories of the delightful years.

Remember, I pray you, that you are in partnership with
all labor—that you should join hands with all the sons and
daughters of toil, and that all who work belong to the same
noble family.

For my part, I envy the man who has lived on the same
broad acres from his boyhood, who cultivates the fields
where in youth he played, and lives where his father lived
and died.

I can imagine no sweeter way to end one's life than in
the quiet of the country, out of the mad race for money,
place and power—far from the demands of business—out of
the dusty highway where fools struggle and strive for the
hollow praise of other fools.

Surrounded by these pleasant fields and faithful friends, by
those I have loved, I hope to end my days.

Little Ones.

—A good way to make children tell the truth is to tell it yourself. Keep your word with your child the same as you would with your banker.

—I intend so to live that when I die my children can come to my grave and truthfully say: "He who sleeps here never gave us one moment of pain." •

—If you tell a child you will do anything, either do it or give the child the reason why. Truth is born of confidence. It comes from the lips of love and liberty.

—We have been saved by that splendid thing called independence, and I want to see more of it, day after day, and I want to see children raised so they will have it. That is my doctrine.

—Make your home happy. Be honest with the children; divide fairly with them in everything. Give them a little liberty, and you cannot drive them out of the house. They will want to stay there. Make home pleasant.

—Let children have some daylight at home if you want to keep them there, and don't commence at the cradle and yell, "Don't!" "Don't!" "Stop!" That is nearly all that is said to a young one from the cradle until he is twenty-one years old.

—Another thing: let the children eat what they want to. Let them commence at whichever end of the dinner they desire. That is my doctrine. They know what they want much better than you do. Nature is a great deal smarter than you ever were.

—Every little while some door is thrown open in some orphan asylum, and there we see the bleeding back of a child whipped beneath the roof that was raised by love. It is infamous, and the man that can't raise a child without the whip ought not to have a child.

—Don't plant your children in long, straight rows, like posts. Let them have light and air, and let them grow beautiful as palms. When I was a little boy, children went to bed when they were not sleepy, and always got up when they were. I would like to see that changed, but they say we are too poor, some of us, to do it. Well, all right. It is as easy to wake a child with a kiss as with a blow; with kindness as with a curse.

—I tell you there is something splendid in man that will not always mind. Why, if we had done as the kings told us five hundred years ago, we would all have been slaves. If we had done as the priests told us, we would all have been idiots. If we had done as the doctors told us, we would all have been dead. We have been saved by disobedience. We have been saved by that splendid thing called independence, and I want to see more of it, day after day, and I want to see children raised so they will have it. That is my doctrine. Give the children a chance.

—Be perfectly honor bright with your children, and they will be your friends when you are old. Don't try to teach

them something they can never learn. Don't insist upon
their pursuing some calling they have no sort of faculty
for. Don't make that poor girl play ten years on a piano
when she has no ear for music, and when she has practiced
until she can play "Bonaparte crossing the Alps," you
can't tell after she has played it whether Bonaparte ever
got across or not. Men are oaks, women are vines, children are flowers, and if there is any Heaven in this world,
it is in the family. It is where the wife loves the husband,
and the husband loves the wife, and where the dimpled
arms of children are about the necks of both.

—If there is one of you here that ever expect to whip your
child again, let me ask you something. Have your photograph taken at the time and let it show your face red with
vulgar anger, and the face of the little one with eyes swim-
ming in tears, and the little chin dimpled with fear, looking like a piece of water struck by a sudden cold wind. If
that little child should die, I cannot think of a sweeter way
to spend an Autumn afternoon than to take that photograph
and go to the cemetery, when the maples are clad in tender
gold, and when little scarlet runners are coming, like poems
of regret, from the sad heart of the earth; and sit down
upon that mound, and look upon that photograph, and
think of the flesh, now dust, that you beat. Just think of
it. I could not bear to die in the arms of a child that I
had whipped. I could not bear to feel upon my lips, when
they were withered beneath the touch of death, the kiss of
one that I had struck.

—I said, and I say again, no day can be so sacred but that
the laugh of a child will make the holiest day more sacred
still. Strike with hand of fire, oh, wierd musician, thy
harp, strung with Apollo's golden hair; fill the vast cathe-
dral aisles with symphonies sweet and dim, deft toucher of

the organ keys; blow, bugler, blow, until thy silver notes
do touch the skies, with moonlit waves, and charm the
lovers wandering on the vine-clad hills: but know, your
sweetest strains are discords all, compared with childhood's
happy laugh, the laugh that fills the eyes with light and
every heart with joy; oh, rippling river of life, thou art
the blessed boundary-line between the beasts and man, and
every wayward wave of thine doth drown some fiend of
care; oh, laughter, divine daughter of joy, make dimples
enough in the cheeks of the world to catch and hold and
glorify all the tears of grief.

—I like to hear children at the table telling what big things
they have seen during the day; I like to hear their merry
voices mingling with the clatter of knives and forks. I had
rather hear that than any opera that was ever put upon the
stage. I hate this idea of authority. I hate dignity. I
never saw a dignified man that was not after all an old
idiot. Dignity is a mask; a dignified man is afraid that
you will know he does not know everything. A man of
sense and argument is always willing to admit what he
don't know—why?—because there is so much that he does
know; and that is the first step towards learning anything
—willingness to admit what you don't know, and when you
don't understand a thing, ask—no matter how small and
silly it may look to other people—ask, and after that you
know. A man never is in a state of mind that he can
learn until he gets that dignified nonsense out of him, and
so I say let us treat our children with perfect kindness and
tenderness.

—I want to tell you that you cannot get the robe of hypocrisy on you so thick that the sharp eye of childhood will
not see through every veil, and if you pretend to your children that you are the best man that ever lived—the bravest

man that ever lived—they will find you out every time. They will not have the same opinion of father when they grow up that they used to have. They will have to be in mighty bad luck if they ever do meaner things than you have done. When your child confesses to you that it has committed a fault, take that child in your arms, and let it feel your heart beat against its heart, and raise your chil· dren in the sunlight of love, and they will be sunbeams to you along the pathway of life. Abolish the club and the whip from the house, because, if the civilized use a whip, the ignorant and the brutal will use a club, and they will use it because you use the whip.

—I was over in Michigan the other day. There was a boy over there at Grand Rapids about five or six years old, a nice, smart boy, as you will see from the remark he made —what you might call a nineteenth century boy. His father and mother had promised to take him out riding. They had promised to take him out riding for about three weeks, and they would slip off and go without him. Well, after a while that got kind of played out with the little boy, and the day before I was there they played the trick on him again. They went out and got the carriage, and went away, and as they rode away from the front of the house, he happened to be standing there with his nurse, and he saw them. The whole thing flashed on him in a moment. He took in the situation, and turned to his nurse and said, pointing to his father and mother: "There goes the two biggest liars in the State of Michigan!" When you go home fill the house with joy, so that the light of it will stream out the windows and doors, and illuminate even the darkness. It is just as easy that way as any in the world.

Ingersoll's Eloquent Speech to the Volunteer Soldiers.

At the banquet given to the Army of the Tennessee, at Chicago, Nov. 13th 18 · , Gen. Sherman announced the following toast: "The volunteer soldiers of the Union army, whose valor and patriotism saved the world a government of the people, by the people and for the people." Response by Col. Robert G. Ingersoll.

Col. Ingersoll, mounting the table by which he was sitting, spoke as follows :

"When the savagery of the lash, the barbarism of the class, and the insanity of secession confronted the civilization of our century, the question, "Will the great republic defend itself?" trembled on the lips of every lover of mankind.

The North, filled with intelligence and wealth—children of liberty—marshalled her hosts and asked only for a leader. From civil life, a man, silent, thoughtful, poised and calm, stepped forth and with lips of victory voiced the nation's first and last demand: "Unconditional and immediate surrender." From that moment the end was known. That utterance was the first real declaration of war, and, in accordance with the dramatic unities of mighty events, the

great soldier who made it received the final reward of the
rebellion.

The soldiers of the republic were not seekers after vulgar
glory. They were not animated by the hope of plunder or
the love of conquest. They fought to preserve the blessings of liberty and that their children might have peace.
They were the defenders of humanity, the destroyers of
prejudice, the breakers of chains, and in the name of the
future they slew the monster of their time. They finished
what the soldiers of the Revolution commenced. They re-
lighted the torch that fell from their august hands and filled
the world again with light. They blotted from the statute
books laws that had been passed by hypocrites at the insti-
gation of robbers, and tore with indignant hands from the
Constitution that infamous clause that made men the catch-
ers of their fellow men.

They made it possible for judges to be just, for statesmen to be human, and for politicians to be honest.

They broke the shackles from the limbs of slaves, from
the souls of martyrs, and from the Northern brain. They

kept our country on the map of the world and our flag in
heaven.

They rolled the stone from the sepulchre of progress,
and for these two angels clad in shining garments—Nation-
ality and Liberty. The soldiers were the saviors of the nation. They were the liberators of men. In writing the

proclamation of independence, Lincoln, the greatest of our mighty dead, whose memory is as gentle as the summer air when reapers sing amid the gathered sheaves—copied with the pen what Grant and his brave comrades wrote with their swords.

Grander than the Greek, nobler than the Roman, the soldiers of the republic, with patriotism as taintless as the air, battled for the rights of others; for the nobility of labor; fought that mothers might own their babes; that arrogant idleness should not scar the back of patient toil, and that our country should not be a many-headed monster made of warring States, but a nation, sovereign, great and free.

Blood was water, money, leaves, and life was common air until one flag floated over a republic without a master and without a slave. Then was asked the question: Will a free people tax themselves to pay the nation's debt?

The soldiers went home to their waiting wives, to their glad children, and to the girls they loved—they went back to the fields, the shops and mines. They had not been de-moralized. They had been ennobled. They were as honest in peace as they had been brave in war. Mocking at poverty, laughing at reverses, they made a friend of toil. They said: "We saved the nation's life, and what is life without honor?" They worked and wrought with all of labor's sons, that every pledge the nation gave should be redeemed. And their great leader, having put a shining hand of friendship—a girdle of clasped and happy hands—around the globe, comes home and finds that every promise made in war has now the ring and gleam of gold.

There is still another question: "Will all the wounds of the war be healed?" I answer, Yes. The Southern peo-ple must submit, not to the dictation of the North, but to the nation's will and to the verdict of mankind. They were wrong, and the time will come when they will say

that they are victors who have been vanquished by the
right. Freedom conquered them, and freedom will cultivate their fields, educate their children, weave for them the
robes of wealth, execute their laws, and fill their land with
happy homes.

The soldiers of the Union saved the South as well as the
North. They made us a Nation. Their victory made us
free and rendered tyranny in every other land as insecure
as snow upon volcano lips.

And now let us drink to the volunteers, to those who
sleep in unknown, sunken graves, whose names are only in
the hearts of those they loved and left—of those who only
hear in happy dreams the footsteps of return.

Let us drink to those who died where lipless famine
mocked at want—to all the maimed whose scars give mod-
esty a tongue, to all who dared and gave to chance the
care and keeping of their lives—to all the living and all the
dead—to Sherman, to Sheridan and to Grant, the foremost
soldiers of the world ; and last, to Lincoln, whose loving
life, like a bow of peace, spans and arches all the clouds of
war."

Honest Money.

I am next in favor of honest money. I am in favor of
gold and silver, and paper with gold and silver behind it.
I believe in silver, because it is one of the greatest of
American products, and I am in favor of anything that will
add to the value of American products. But I want a silver
dollar worth a gold dollar, even if you make it or have to
make it four feet in diameter. No Government can afford
to be a clipper of coin. A great Republic cannot afford to
stamp a lie upon silver or gold. Honest money, an honest
people, an honest Nation. When our money is only worth

80 cents on the dollar, we feel 20 per cent. below par.
When our money is good we feel good.   When our money
is at par, that is where we are.   I am a profound believer
in the doctrine that for nations.as well as men, honesty is
the best, always, everywhere and forever.

Eloquent Defense of Good Government.

We all want a good Government.   If we do not, we
should have none.   We all want to live in a land where
the law is supreme.   We desire to live beneath a flag that
will protect every citizen beneath its folds.   We desire to be
citizens of a Government so great and so grand that it will
command the respect of the civilized world.

Most of us are convinced that our Government is the best
upon this earth.

It is the only Government where manhood, and manhood alone, is made not simply a condition of citizenship, but where manhood, and manhood alone, permits its possessor to have his equal share in the control of the Government. It is the only Government where poverty is upon an exact equality with wealth, so far as controlling the destinies of the Republic is concerned.

It is the only Nation where the man clothed in a rag stands upon an equality with the one wearing purple.

It is the only country in the world where, politically, the hut is upon an equality with the palace.

For that reason, every poor man should stand by that Government, and every poor man who does not is a traitor to the best interests of his children; every poor man who does not is willing his children should bear the badge of political inferiority; and the only way to make this Government a complete and perfect success is for the poorest man to think as much of his manhood as the millionaire does of his wealth.

A man does not vote in this country simply because he is rich; he does not vote in this country simply because he has an education; he does not vote simply because he has talent or genius; we say that he votes because he is a man, and that he has his manhood to support; and we admit in this country that nothing can be more valuable to any human being than his manhood, and for that reason we put poverty on an equality with wealth.

We say in this country manhood is worth more than gold. We say in this country that without liberty the Nation is not worth preserving. I appeal to every laboring man, and I ask him, Is there another country on this globe where you can have your equal rights with others? Now, then, in every country, no matter how good it is, and no matter how bad it is—in every country there is something worth preserving, and there is something that ought to be destroyed. Now recollect that every voter is in his own right a king; every voter in this country wears a crown; every voter in this country has in his hands the scepter of authority; and every voter, poor and rich, wears the purple of author. ity alike. Recollect it; and the man that will sell his vote is the man that abdicates the American throne.

The man that sells his vote strips himself of the imperial purple, throws away the scepter, and admits that he is less than a man. More than that, the man that will sell his vote for prejudice or for hatred, the man that will be lied out of his vote, that will be slandered out of his vote, that will be fooled out of his vote, is not worthy to be an American citizen.

Now let us understand ourselves. Let us endeavor to do what is right; let us say this country is good—we will make it better; let us say if our children do not live in a Republic it shall not be our fault.

A Picture.

The other night I happened to notice a sunset. The sun went down, and the west was full of light and fire, and I said: "There is the perfect death of a great man; that dying sun leaves a legacy of glory to the very clouds that obstruct its path. That sun, like a great man, dying, leaves a legacy of glory even to the ones who persecuted him, and the world is glorious only because there have been men great enough and grand enough to die for the right." Will any man, can any man afford to die for this country? Then we can afford to vote for it. If a man can afford to fight for it and die for it, I can afford to speak for it.

And now I beg of you, every man and woman, no matter in what country born,—if you are an Irishman, recol-

lect that this country has done more for your race than all
other countries under heavens; if you are a German, recollect that this country is kinder to you than your own fath-
erland,—no matter what country you came from, remember that this country is an asylum, and vote as in your
conscience you believe you ought to vote to keep this flag
in heaven. I beg every American to stand with that part
of the country that believes in law, in freedom of speech,
in an honest vote, in civilization, in progress, in human
liberty, and in universal justice.

Good Dollars and Good Times.

If I am fortunate enough to leave a dollar when I die,
I want it to be a good one ; I don't wish to have it turn to
ashes in the hands of widowhood, or because a Democratic
broken promise in the pocket of the orphan ; I want it
money. I saw not long ago a piece of gold bearing the
stamp of the Roman Empire. That Empire is dust, and
over it has been thrown the mantle of oblivion, but that
piece of gold is as good as though Julius Cæsar were still
riding at the head of the Roman Legion. I want money
that will outlive the Democratic party. They told us—
and they were honest about it—they said, "when we
have plenty of money, we are prosperous." And I
said : "When we are prosperous, then we have credit, and,
credit inflates the currency. Whenever a man buys a
pound of sugar and says, 'Charge it,' he inflates the currency ; whenever he gives his note, he inflates the currency; whenever his word takes the place of money, he
inflates the currency." The consequence is that when we
are prosperous, credit takes the place of money, and we
have what we call "plenty." But you can't increase prosperity simply by using promises to pay.

Suppose you should come to a river that was about dry, and there you would see the ferryboat, and the gentleman who kept the ferry, high on the sand, and the cracks all opening in the sun filled with loose oakum, looking like an average Democratic mouth listening to a Constitutional argument, and you should say to him:

"How is business?"

He would say " Dull."

And then you would say to him, "Now, what you want is more boat."

He would probably answer, "If I had a little more water I could get along with this one."

Ingersoll's Apt Words on State Lines.

In old times, in the year of grace, 1860, if a man wished the army of the United States to pursue a fugitive slave, then the army could cross a State line. Whenever it has been necessary to deprive some human being of a right, then we had a right to cross State lines; but whenever we wished to strike the shackles of slavery from a human being we had no right to cross a State line. In other words, when you want to do a mean thing you can step over the line, but if your object is a good one you shall not do it.

This doctrine of State sovereignty is the meanest doctrine that was ever lodged in the American mind. It is political poison, and if this country is destroyed that doctrine will have done as much toward it as any other one thing. I believe the Union one absolutely. The Democrat tells me that when I am away from home the Government will protect me; but when I am home, when I am sitting around the family fireside of the nation, then the Government cannot protect me; that I must leave if I want protection. Now I denounce that doctrine. For instance, we are at war with another country, and the American nation comes to me and says : "·We want you."

I say : ' I won't go."

They draft me, put some names in a wheel, and a man turns it and another man pulls out a paper, and my name is on it, and he says : "Come." So I go, and I fight for the flag. When the war is over I go back to my State. Now let us adm.. 'hat the war has been unpopular, and that when I got to the State the people of that State wished to trample upon my rights, and I cried out to my Government: "Come and defend me ; you made me defend you." What ought the Government to do ?

I only owe that Government allegiance that owes me my protection. Protection is the other side of the bargain ; that is what it must be. And if a Government ought to protect even the man that it drafts, what ought it to do for the volunteer, the man who holds his wife for a moment in a tremulous embrace, and kisses his children, wets their cheeks with his tears, shoulders his musket, goes to the field, and says : "Here I am to uphold my flag." A nation that will not protect such a protector is a disgrace to mankind, and its flag a dirty rag that contaminates the air in which it waves.

I believe in a Government with an arm long enough to reach the collar of any rascal beneath its flag.

I want it with an arm long enough and a sword sharp enough to strike down tyranny wherever it may raise its snaky head.

I want a nation that can hear the faintest cries of its humblest citizen.

I want a nation that will protect a freedman standing in the sun by his little cabin, just as quick as it would protect Vanderbilt in a palace of marble and gold.

I believe in a Government that can cross a State line on an

errand of mercy.   I believe in a Government that can cross
a State line when it wishes to do justice.   I do not believe
that the sword turns to air at a State line.   I want a Government that will protect me.   I am here (Rockford, Ill.,)
to-day—do I stand here because the flag of Illinois is above
me ?   I want no flag of Illinois, and if I were to see it I

should not know it.   I am here to-day under the folds of
the flag of my country, for which more good, blessed blood
has been shed than for any other flag that waves in this
world.   I have as much right to speak here as if I had been
born right here.

That is the country in which I believe ; that is the nation
that commands my respect, that protects all.

Ingersollisms.

᠆ The thoughts of a man who is not free are not worth much—not much.

— We have a common interest in the preservation of a common country.

—I believe in absolute intellectual liberty; that a man has a right to think.

—I never knew a man who did a decent action that wanted it forgotten.

—It will be thousands of years before the world will be willing to say that right makes might.

—I had rather be a beggar and spend my last dollar like

a king than be a king and spend my money like a beggar.

—If you want to get at the honest thoughts of a man he must be free. If he is not free you will not get his honest thought.

—Whenever a man does what mantles the cheeks of his children with shame, he is the man who says, "Let by-gones be by-gones."

—The Constitution of the United States was the first decree entered in the high court of a nation forever divorc-ing Church and State.

—Printing gave pinions to thought and made it possible for man to bequeath to the future the richness of his brain, the wealth of his soul.

—I believe another thing. If I belong to the superior race I will be so superior that I can make my living without stealing from the inferior.

—We used to worship the golden calf, and the worst you can say of us now, is, we worship the gold of the calf, and even the calves are beginning to see this distinction.

—Education is the most radical thing in the world. To teach the alphabet is to inaugurate a revolution. To build a school house is to construct a fort. A library is an arsenal.

—I say here that I think a hundred times more of the good, honest, black, industrious man of the South than I do of all the white men together that don't love the government.

—In the long run the nation that is honest, the people that are industrious, will pass the people that are dishonest, the people that are idle; no matter what grand ancestry they may have had.

—I believe that every round in the ladder of fame, from the one that rests on the ground to the last one that leaps against the shining summit of human ambition, belongs to the foot that gets on it.

—Every man who has invented anything for the use and convenience of man has helped raise his fellow man.

—You should keep your minds open to reason; hear what a man has to say, and do not let the turtle-shell of bigotry grow above your brain. Give everybody a chance and an opportunity ; that is all.

—If some men were as ashamed of appearing cross in public as they are of appearing tender at home, this world would be infinitely better. I think you can make your home a heaven if you want to—you can make up your minds to that.

—I believe if you have got a dollar in the world and you have got to spend it, spend it like a man ; spend it like a king, like a prince. If you have to spend it, spend it as though it was a dried leaf, and you were the owner of un-bounded forests.

—The last Napoleon was not satisfied with being Emperor of the French; he was not satisfied with having a circlet of gold about his head ; he wanted some one evidence that he had something within his head, so he wrote the life of Julius Cæsar, that he might become a member of the French academy.

—In every age some men carried the torch of progress and handed it to some other, and it has been carried through all the dark ages of barbarism, and had it not been for such men we would have been naked and uncivilized to-night, with pictures of wild beasts tattooed on our skins, dancing around some dried snake fetish.

—The more a man knows the more liberal he is ; the less a man knows the more bigoted he is. The less a man knows the more certain he is that he knows it, and the more a man knows the better satisfied he is that he is entirely ignorant. Great knowledge is philosophic, and little, narrow, contemptible knowledge is bigoted and hateful.

—I have sometimes wished that there were words of pure hatred out of which I might construct sentences like snakes, out of which I might construct sentences with mouths fanged, that had forked tongues, out of which I might construct sentences that writhed and hissed; then I could give my opinion of the rebels during the great struggle for the preservation of this nation.

—The grave is not a throne, and a corpse is not a king. The living have a right to control this world. I think a good deal more of to-day than I do of yesterday, and I think more of to-morrow than I do of this day; because, it is nearly gone—that is the way I feel. The time to be happy is now; the way to be happy is to make somebody else happy and the place to be happy is here.

—It is not necessary to be rich, nor powerful, nor great to be a success; and neither is it necessary to have your name between the putrid lips of rumor to be great. We have had a false standard of success. In the years when I was a little boy we read in our books that no fellow was a success that did not make a fortune or get a big office, and he generally was a man that slept about three hours a night. They never put down in the books the names of those gentlemen that succeeded in life that slept all they wanted to; and we all thought that we could not sleep to exceed three or four hours if we ever expected to be anything in this world. We have had a wrong standard.

The Celebrated Speech of Col. Ingersoll Nominating James G. Blaine for President.

At Cincinnati, June, 1876, in nominating James G. Blaine for President, Col. Ingersoll spoke as follows: (full report.)

MR. CHAIRMAN, LADIES AND GENTLEMEN: Massachusetts may be satisfied with the loyalty of Benjamin H. Bristow; so am I; but if any man nominated by this convention cannot carry the State of Massachusetts, I am not satisfied with the loyalty of that State. If the nominee of this convention cannot carry the grand old commonwealth of Massachusetts by seventy-five thousand majority I would advise them to sell out Faneuil Hall as a Democratic headquarters. I would advise them to take from Bunker Hill that old monument of glory.

The Republicans of the United States demand as their leader in the great contest of 1876, a man of intelligence, a man of integrity, a man of well-known and approved political opinions. They demand a statesman; they demand a reformer after as well as before the election. They demand a politician in the highest, broadest and best sense—a man of superb moral courage. They demand a man acquainted with public affairs; with the wants of the people; with not only the requirements of the hour, but with the demands of the future.

They demand a man broad enough to comprehend the relations of this Government to the other nations of the earth. They demand a man well versed in the powers, duties and prerogatives of each and every department of this Government. They demand a man who will sacredly preserve the financial honor of the United States; one who knows enough to know that the national debt must be paid through the prosperity of the people; one who knows enough to know that all the financial theories in the world cannot redeem a single dollar; one who knows enough to know that all the money must be made, not by law but by labor; one who knows enough to know that the people of the United States have the industry to make the money, and the honor to pay it over just as fast as they make it.

The Republicans of the United States demand a man who knows that prosperity and resumption, when they come, must come together; that when they come they will come hand in hand through the golden harvest fields; hand in hand by the whirling spindles and the turning wheels; hand in hand past the open furnace doors; hand in hand by the chimneys filled with eager fire, greeted and grasped by the countless sons of toil.

This money has to be dug out of the earth. You cannot make it by passing resolutions in a political convention.

The Republicans of the United States want a man who knows that this Government should protect every citizen, at home and abroad; who knows that any Government that will not defend its defenders and protect its protectors, is a disgrace to the map of the world. They demand a man who believes in the eternal separation and divorcement of church and school. They demand a man whose political reputation is as spotless as a star; but they do not demand that their candidate shall have a certificate of moral character signed by a Confederate Congress. The man who has, in full, heaped and rounded measure, all these splendid qualifications is the present grand and gallant leader of the Republican party—James G. Blaine.

Our country, crowned with the vast and marvelous achievements of its first century, asks for a man worthy of the past and prophetic of her future; asks for a man who has the audacity of genius; asks for a man who is the grandest combination of heart, conscience and brain beneath her flag. Such a man is James G. Blaine.

For the Republican host, led by this intrepid man, there can be no defeat.

This is a grand year—a year filled with recollections of the Revolution ; filled with the proud and tender memories of the past; with the sacred legends of liberty ; a year in which the sons of freedom will drink from the fountains of enthusiasm ; a year in which the people call for a man who has preserved in Congress what our soldiers won upon the field ; a year in which they call for the man who has torn from the throat of treason the tongue of slander—for the man who has snatched the mask of Democracy from the hideous face of rebellion ; for this man who, like an intellectual athlete, has stood in the arena of debate and challenged all comers, and who is still a total stranger to defeat.

Like an armed warrior, like a plumed knight, James G. Blaine marched down the halls of the American Congress and threw his shining lance full and fair against the brazen foreheads of the defamers of his country and the maligners of her honor. For the Republican party to desert this gallant leader now is as though an army should desert their General upon the field of battle.

James G. Blaine is now and has been for years the bearer of the sacred standard of the Republican party. I call it sacred because no human being can stand beneath its folds without becoming and without remaining free.

Gentlemen of the convention, in the name of the great Republic, the only Republic that ever existed upon this earth ; in the name of all her defenders and of all her supporters ; in the name of all her soldiers living ; in the name of all her soldiers dead upon the field of battle, and in the name of those who perished in the skeleton clutch of famine at Andersonville and Libby, whose sufferings he so vividly remembers, Illinois—Illinois nominates for the next

President of this country that prince of parliamentarians—
that leader of leaders—James G. Blaine.

A Country Full of Kings.

I want the power where somebody can use it.   As long
as a man is responsible to the people there is no fear of despotism.   There's no reigning family in this country.   We
are all of us Kings.   We are the reigning family.   And
when any man talks about despotism, you may be sure he
wants to steal or be up to devilment.   If we have any sense,
we have got to have localization of brain.   If we have any
power, we must have centralization.   We want centralization of the right kind.   The man we choose for our head

wants the army in one hand and the navy in the other, and to execute the supreme will of the supreme people.

But you say you will cross a State line. I hope so. When the Democratic party was in power and wanted to pursue a human slave, there was no State line. When we want to save a human being, the State line rises up like a Chinese wall. I believe when one party can cross a State line to put a chain on, another party can cross it to take a chain off. "Why," you say, "you want the Federal Government to interfere with the rights of a State." Yes, I do, if necessary. I want the ear of the Government acute enough and arm long enough to reach a wronged man in any State. A government that will not protect its protectors is no government. Its flag is a dirty rag. That is not my government. I want a government that will protect its citizens at home. The Democratic doctrine is that a government can only protect its citizens abroad. If a father can't protect his children at home, depend upon it, that he can't do much for them when they are abroad.

Think of it! Here's a war. They come to me in Illinois and draft me. They tell me I must go. I go through the war and come home safe. Afterwards that State finds a way to trample on me. I say to the Federal Government, "You told me I owed my first allegiance to you, and I had to go to war. Now, I say to you, You owe your first allegiance to me, and I want you to protect me!

The Federal Government says, "Oh, you must ask your State to request it."

I say, "That's just what they won't do!" · Such a condition of things is perfectly horrible!

If so with a man who was drafted, what will you say of a volunteer? Yet that's the Democratic doctrine of Federal Government. It won't do! And you know it!

Some Laughable Remarks About Money With a Few Illustrations.

They say that money is a measure of value. 'Tisn't so. A bushel doesn't measure values. It measures diamonds as well as potatoes. If it measured values, a bushel of potatoes would be worth as much as a bushel of diamonds. A yard-stick doesn't measure values. They used to say, "there's no use in having a gold yard-stick." That was right. You don't buy the yard-stick. If money bore the same relation to trade as a yard-stick or half-bushel, you would have the same money when you got through trading as you had when you begun. A man don't sell half-bushels. He sells corn. All we want is a little sense about these things.

I don't blame the man who wanted inflation. I don't blame him for praying for another period of inflation. "When it comes," said the man who had a lot of shrunken property on his hands, "blame me, if I don't unload, you may shoot me." It's a good deal like the game of poker! I don't suppose any of you know anything about that game! Along towards morning the fellow who is ahead always wants another deal. The fellow that is behind says his wife's sick, and he must go home. You ought to hear that fellow descant on domestic virtue! And the other fellow accuses him of being a coward and wanting to jump the game. A man whose dead wood is hung up on the shore in a dry time, wants the water to rise once more and float it out into the middle of the stream.

We were in trouble. The thing was discussed. Some said there wasn't enough money. That's so; I know what that means myself. They said if we had more money we'd be more prosperous. The truth is, if we were more prosperous we'd have more money. They said more money would facilitate business.

Suppose a shareholder in a railroad that had earned $18,000 the past year should look over the books and find that in that year the railroad had used $12,000 worth of grease. The next year, suppose the earnings should fall off $5,000, and the man, in looking over the accounts, should learn that in that year the road had used only $500 worth of grease! Supposing the man should say: "The trouble is, we want more grease." What would you think of a man if he discharged the superintendent for not using more grease?

I said, years ago, that resumption would come only by prosperity, and the only way to pay debts was by labor. I knew that every man who raised a bushel of corn helped resumption. It was a question of crops, a question of industry.

An Amusing Story.

ou Greenbackers are like the old woman in the Tewksbury, Mass., Poor-House. She used to be well off, and didn't like her quarters. You Greenbackers have left your father's house of many mansions and have fed on shucks about long enough. The Supervisor came into the Poor-House one day and asked the old lady how she liked it. She said she didn't like the company, and asked him what he would advise her to do under similar circumstances.

"Oh, you'd better stay. You're prejudiced," said he.

"Do you think anybody is ever prejudiced in their sleep?" asked the old lady. "I had a dream the other night. I dreamed I died and went to Heaven. Lots of nice people were there. A nice man came to me and asked me where I was from. Says I, 'From Tewksbury, Mass.'

He looked in his book and said, "You can't stay here."

"I asked what he would advise me to do under similar circumstances.

"'Well,' he said, 'there's Hell down there, you might try that.'

"Well, I went down there, and the man told me my name wasn't on the book and I couldn't stay there. 'Well,' said I, "What would you advise me to do under similar circumstances?'

"Said he, 'You'll have to go back to Tewksbury.'"

And when Greenbackers remember what they once were, you must feel now, when you were forced to join the Democratic party, as bad as the old lady who had to go back to Tewksbury.

Money and Yardsticks.

A thousand theories were born of want; a thousand theories were born of the fertile brain of trouble; and these people said after all: "What is money? why it is nothing but a measure of value, just the same as a half-bushel or yardstick." True. And consequently it makes no difference whether your half-bushel is of wood, or gold, or silver, or paper; and it makes no difference whether your yardstick is gold or paper. But the trouble about that statement is this: A half-bushel is not a measure of value; it is a measure of quantity, and it measures rubies, diamonds and pearls, precisely the same as corn and wheat. The yardstick is not a measure of value; it is a measure of length, and it measures lace, worth $100 a yard, precisely as it does cent tape. And another reason why it makes no difference to the purchaser whether the half-bushel is gold or silver, or whether the yardstick is gold or paper, you don't buy the yardstick; you don't get the half-bushel in the trade. And if it was so with money—if the people

that had the money at the start of the trade, kept it after
the consummation of the bargain—then it wouldn't make
any difference what you made your money of. But the
trouble is, the money changes hands. And let me say right
here, money is a thing—it is a product of nature--and you
can no more make a "fiat" dollar than you can make a fiat
star.

Bright Money.

Now listen: No civilized nation, no barbarous nation,
no tribe, however ignorant, ever used anything as money
that man could make. They had always used for money
a production of nature. Some may say, "Have not some
uncivilized tribes used beads for money, something that
civilized people could make?" Yes, but a savage tribe
could not make the beads. The savage tribes supposed
them to be a product either of nature or of something else
that they could not imitate.

Nothing has ever been considered money among any
people on this globe that those people could make. What
is a greenback? The greenbacks are a promise, not money.
The greenbacks are the nation's note, not money. You
cannot make a fiat dollar any more than you can make a
fiat store. You can make a promise, and that promise
may be made by such a splendid man that it will pass
among all who know him as a dollar; but it is not a dollar.
You might as well tell me that a bill of fare is a dinner.
The greenback is only good now because you can get gold
for it. If you could not get gold for it it would not be
worth any more than a ticket for dinner after the fellow
who issued the ticket had quit keeping the hotel. A dollar
must be made of something that nature has produced.

When I die, if I have a dollar left I want it to be a good

one. I do not want a dollar that will turn into ashes in the hand of widowhood or in the possession of an orphan. Take a coin of the Roman empire—a little piece of gold—and it is just as good to-day as though Julius Cæsar still stood at. the head of the Roman legions. I do not wish to trust the wealth of this nation with the demagogs of the nation. I do not wish to trust the wealth of the country to every blast of public opinion. I want money as solid as the earth on which we tread, as bright as the stars that shine above us.

A Panic Picture.

No man can imagine, all the languages of the world cannot express what the people of the United States suffered from 1873 to 1879. Men who considered themselves millionaires found that they were beggars; men living in palaces, supposing they had enough to give sunshine to the winter of their age, supposing they had enough to have all they loved in affluence and comfort, suddenly found that they were mendicants with bonds, stocks, mortgages, all turned to ashes in their aged, trembling hands. The chimneys grew cold, the fires in furnaces went out, the poor families were turned adrift, and the highways of the United States were crowded with tramps. Into the home of the poor crept the serpent of temptation, and whispered in the ear of poverty the terrible word "repudiation."

I want to tell you that you cannot conceive of what the American people suffered as they staggered over the desert of bankruptcy from 1873 to 1879. We are too near now to know how grand we were. The poor mechanics said "No;" the ruined manufacturer said "No;" the once millionaire said "No, we will settle fair; we will agree to pay whether we ever pay or not, and we will never soil the

American name with the infamous word, 'repudiation.'"
Are you not glad? What is the talk? Are you not glad
that our flag is covered all over with financial honors? The
stars shine and gleam now because they represent an honest nation.

Repudiation.

I think there is the greatest heroism in living for a thing!
There's no glory in digging potatoes. You don't wear a
uniform when you're picking up stones. You can't have a
band of music when you dig potatoes! In 1873 came the
great crash. We staggered over the desert of bankruptcy.
No one can estimate the anguish of that time. Millionaires
found themselves paupers. Palaces were exchanged for
hovels. The aged man, who had spent his life in hard
labor, and who thought he had accumulated enough to support himself in his old age, and leave a little something to
his children and grandchildren, found they were all beggars.
The highways were filled with tramps.

Then it was that the serpent of temptation whispered in
the ear of want that dreadful word "Repudiation." ·An
effort was made to repudiate. They appealed to want, to
misery, to threatened financial ruin, to the bare hearth-
stones, to the army of beggars. We had grandeur enough
to say: "No; we'll settle fair if we don't pay a cent!"
And we'll pay it. 'Twas grandeur! Is there a Democrat
now who wishes we had taken the advice of Bayard to
scale the bonds? Is there an American, a Democrat here,
who is not glad we escaped the stench and shame of repudiation, and did not take Democratic advice? Is there a
Greenbacker here who is not glad we didn't do it? He
may say he is, but he isn't. We then had to pay 7 per
cent. interest on our bonds. Now we only pay 4. Our

greenbacks were then at 10 per cent. discount. Now they are at par. How would an American feel to be in Germany or France and hear it said that the United States repudiated? We have found out that money is something that can't be made. We have found out that money is a product of Nature. When a nation gets hard up, it is right and proper for it to give its notes, and it should pay them. We have found out that it is better to trust for payment to the miserly cleft of the rocks than to any Congress blown about by the wind of demagogs. We want our money good in any civilized nation. Yes, we want it good in Central Africa! And when a naked Hottentot sees a United States greenback blown about by the wind, he will pick it up as eagerly as if it was a lump of gold. They say even now that money is a device to facilitate exchanges. 'Tisn't so! Gold is not a device. Silver is not a device. You might as well attempt to make fiat suns, moons, and stars as a fiat dollar.

Protection.

There is another thing in which I believe. I believe in the protection of American labor. The hand that holds Aladdin's lamp must be the hand of toil. This nation rests upon the shoulders of its workers, and I want the American laboring man to have enough to wear. I want him to have enough to eat. I want him to have something for the ordinary misfortunes of life. I want him to have the pleasure of seeing his wife well dressed. I want him to see a few blue ribbons fluttering about his children. I want him to see the flags of health flying in their beautiful cheeks. I want him to feel that this is his country, and the shield of protection is above his labor.

And I will tell you why I am for protection, too. If we were all farmers we would be stupid. If we were all shoe makers we would be stupid. If we all followed one busi" ness, no matter what it was, we would become stupid. Protection to American labor diversifies American indus- try, and to have it diversified touches and developes every part of the human brain. Protection protects integrity ; it protects intelligence ; and protection raises sense ; and by protection we have greater men and better-looking women and healthier children. Free trade means that our laborer is upon an equality with the poorest paid labor of this world.

The Tariff.

Where did this doctrine of a tariff for revenue only come from ? From the South. The South would like to stab the prosperity of the North. They had rather trade with Old England than with New England. They had rather trade with the people who were willing to help them in war than those who conquered the rebellion. They knew what gave us our strength in war. They knew that all the brooks and creeks and rivers in New England were putting down the rebellion. They knew that every wheel that turned, every spindle that revolved, was a soldier in the army of human progress. It won't do. They were so lured by the greed of office that they were willing to trade upon the misfortunes of a nation. It won't do. I don't wish to belong to a party that succeeds only when my country falls. I don't wish to belong to a party whose banner went up with the banner of rebellion. I don't wish to belong to a party that was in partnership with defeat and disaster. I don't. And there isn't a Democrat here but what knows that a failure of the crops this year would have helped his party. You know that an early frost would have been a godsend to them. You know that the potatobug could have done them more good than all their speakers.

Ingersoll's History of State Sovereignty.

This doctrine of State sovereignty has to be done away with; we have got to stamp it out. Let me tell you its history: The first time it ever appeared was when they wished to keep the slave trade alive until 1808. The first resort to this doctrine was for the protection of piracy and murder, and the next time they appealed to it was to keep the inter-state slave trade alive, so that a man in Virginia could sell the very woman that nursed him, to the rice fields of the South. It was done so they could raise mankind as a crop. It was a crop that they could thresh the year around.

The next time they appealed to the doctrine was in favor of the Fugitive Slave law, so that every white man in the North was to become a hound to bay upon the track of the fugitive slave. Under that law the North agreed to catch women and give them back to the bloodhounds of the South. Under that infamy men and women were held and were kidnapped under the shadow of the dome of the National Capitol. If the Democratic party had remained in power it would be so now. The South said: " Be friends with us, all we want is to steal labor; be friends with us, all we want of you is to have you catch our slaves; be friends with us, all we want of you is to be in partnership in the business of slavery, and we are to take all the money and you are to have the disgrace and dishonor for your share." The dividend didn't suit me.

The next time they appealed to the doctrine of State rights was that they might extend the area of human slavery; it was that they might desecrate the fair fields of Kansas.

The next time they appealed to this infamous doctrine was in secession and treason; so now, when I hear any man advocate this doctrine, I know that he is not a friend of my country, he is not a friend of humanity, of liberty, or of progress.

A Dark Picture.

This world has not been fit to live in fifty years. There is no liberty in it—very little. Why, it is only a few years ago that all the Christian nations were engaged in the slave trade. It was not until 1808 that England abolished the slave trade, and up to that time her priests in her churches, and her judges on her benches, owned stock in slave ships, and luxuriated on the profits of piracy and murder; and when a man stood up and denounced it, they mobbed him as though he had been a common burglar or a horse thief. Think of it! It was not until the 28th day of August, 1833, that England abolished slavery in her colonies; and it was not until the first day of January, 1862, that Abraham Lincoln by direction of the entire North, wiped that infamy out of this country; and I never speak of Abraham Lincoln but I want to say that he was, in my judgment, in many respects the grandest man ever President of the United States. I say that upon his tomb there ought

to be this line—and I know of no other man deserving it
so well as he: "Here lies one who having been clothed
with almost absolute power never abused it except on the
side of mercy."

What the Colonel Has Seen and What he Wants to See.

I have been in countries where the laboring man had
meat once a year; sometimes twice—Christmas and Easter.
And I have seen women carrying upon their heads a burden that no man would like to carry, and at the same time
knitting busily with both hands. And those women lived
without meat; and when I thought of the American laborer
I said to myself, "After all, my country is the best in the
world." And when I came back to the sea and saw the
old flag flying in the air, it seemed to me as though the air
from pure joy had burst into blossom.

Labor has more to eat and more to wear in the United
States than in any other land of this earth. I want America to produce everything that Americans need. I want it
so if the whole world should declare war against us, so if
we were surrounded by walls of cannons and bayonets and
swords, we could supply all our human wants in and of
ourselves. I want to live to see the American woman
dressed in American silk; the American man in everything
from hat to boots produced in America by the cunning
hand of the American toiler.

I want to see a workingman have a good house, painted
white, grass in the front yard, carpets on the floor and pictures on the wall. I want to see him a man feeling that
he is a king by the divine right of living in the Republic.
And every man here is just a little bit a king, you know.
Every man here is a part of the sovereign power. Every

man wears a little of purple; every man has a little of crown and a little of sceptre; and every man that will sell his vote for money or be ruled by prejudice is unfit to be an American citizen.

The Struggle for Liberty.

Seven long years of war—fighting for what? For the principle that all men are created equal—a truth that nobody ever disputed except a scoundrel; nobody in the entire history of this world. No man ever denied *that* truth who was not a rascal, and at heart a thief; never, never, and never will. What else were they fighting for? Simply that in America every man should have a right to life, liberty and the pursuit of happiness. Nobody ever denied that except a villain; never, never. It has been denied by kings—they were thieves. It has been denied by statesmen—they were liars. It has been denied by priests, by clergymen, by cardinals, by bishops and by popes—they were hypocrites.

What else were they fighting for? For the idea that all political power is vested in the great body of the people. They make all the money; do all the work. They plow the land; cut down the forests; they produce everything that is produced. Then who shall say what shall be done with what is produced, except the producer? Is it the non-producing thief, sitting on a throne, surrounded by vermin?

The history of civilization is the history of the slow and painful enfranchisement of the human race. In the olden times the family was a monarchy, the father being the monarch. The mother and children were the veriest slaves. The will of the father was the supreme law. He had the power of life and death. It took thousands of years to civilize this father, thousands of years to make the condition of wife and mother and children even tolerable. A few families constituted a tribe; the tribe had a chief; the chief was a tyrant; a few tribes formed a nation; the nation was governed by a king, who was also a tyrant. A strong nation robbed, plundered and took captive the weaker ones.

America's Coming Greatness.

Standing here amid the sacred memories of the first century, on the golden threshold of the second, I ask, Will the second century be as grand as the first? I believe it will, because we are growing more and more humane; I believe there is more human kindness, and a greater desire to help one another, than in all the world besides.

We must progress. We are just at the commencement of invention. The steam engine—the telegraph—these are but the toys with which science has been amused. There will be grander things; there will be wider and higher culture—a grander standard of character, of literature and art.

We have now half as many millions of people as we have years. We are getting more real solid sense. We are writing and reading more books; we are struggling more and more to get at the philosophy of life, of things—trying more and more to answer the questions of the eternal Sphinx. We are looking in every direction—investigating; in short, we are thinking and working.

The world has changed. I have had the supreme pleasure of seeing a man—once a slave—sitting in the seat of his former master in the Congress of the United States. I have had that pleasure, and when I saw it my eyes were filled with tears, I felt that we had carried out the Declaration of Independence, that we had given reality to it, and breathed the breath of life into its every word. I felt that our flag would float over and protect the colored man and his little children—standing straight in the sun, just the same as though he were white and worth a million.

All who stand beneath our banner are free. Ours is the only flag that has in reality written upon it: Liberty, Fraternity, Equality—the three grandest words in all the languages of men. Liberty: Give to every man the fruit of his own labor—the labor of his hand and of his brain. Fraternity: Every man in the right is my brother. Equality: The rights of all are equal. No race, no color, no previous condition, can change the rights of men. The Declaration of Independence has at last been carried out in letter and in spirit. The second century will be grander than the first. To-day the black man looks upon his child and says: The avenues of distinction are open to you—upon your brow may fall the civic wreath. We are celebrating the courage and wisdom of our fathers, and the glad shout of a free people, the anthem of a grand nation, commencing at the Atlantic, is following the sun to the Pacific, across a continent of happy homes. We are a great people. Three millions have increased to fifty—thirteen states to thirty-eight. We have better homes, and more of the conveniences of life than any other people upon the face of the globe. The farmers of our country live better than did the kings and princes two hundred years ago—and they have twice as much sense and heart. Liberty and labor have given us all. Remember that all men have equal rights. Remember that the man who acts best his part—who loves his friends the best—is most willing to help others—truest to the obligation—who has the best heart—the most feeling—the deepest sympathies—and who freely gives to others the rights that he claims for himself, is the best man. We have disfranchised the aristocrats of the air and have given one country to mankind.

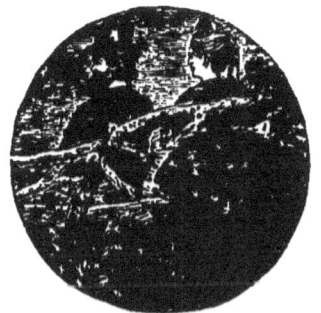

Ingersollisms.

—Musicians playing to a deaf audience will not do their best.

—Man must give liberty to others if he would be free himself.

—A lie will not fit a fact; it will only fit another lie for the purpose.

—For ages reason was the cry of a drowning man lost in the roaring sea.

—Every fact pushes a superstition from the brain and a ghost from the clouds.

—Fear paints pictures of the ghosts and hangs them in the gallery of ignorance.

—The man who does not do his own thinking is a slave, and does not do his duty to his fellow-men.

—Every form of slavery is a viper that will sooner or later strike its poisonous fangs into the bosoms of man.

—Out on the intellectual sea there is room for every sail; in the intellectual air there is space enough for every wing.

—Without liberty there can be no worship. The slave may bow, and cringe, and crawl, but he cannot live, he cannot adore.

—Great minds seem to be a part of the infinite. Those possessing them seem to be brothers of the mountains and the seas.

—And this is my advice to the poor. You can never be so poor that whatever you do you can't do in a grand and manly way.

—Frederick Douglass told me that he had lectured upon the subject of freedom twenty years before he was permitted to set his foot in a church.

—The time is coming when a man will be rated at his real worth, and that by his brain and heart. We care nothing now about an officer unless he fills his place.

—The time will come when no matter how much money a man has he will not be respected unless he is using it for the benefit of his fellow-men. It will soon be here.

—I pity the man, I execrate the man, who has only to brag that he is white. Whenever I am reduced to that necessity, I believe shame will make me red instead of white

—Great men do not live alone; they are surrounded by the great; they are the instruments used to accomplish the tendencies of their generation; they fulfil the prophecies of their age.

—I believe all the intellectual domain of the future is open to every man. Every man who finds a fact first, that is to be his fact. Every man who thinks a thought first, that is to be his thought.

—I know not what discoveries, what inventions, what thoughts may leap from the brain of the world. I know not what garments of glory may be woven by the years to come. I cannot dream of the victories to be won upon the field of thought; but I do know that, coming down the infinite sea of the future, there will never touch this "bank and shoal of time" a richer gift, a rarer blessing than liberty for man, woman and child.

—I believe in liberty, and I say, "Oh, liberty, float not forever in the far horizon—remain not forever in the dream of the enthusiast, the philanthropist and poet, but come and make thy home among the children of men."

—All the mechanical ingenuity of this earth cannot make two clocks run alike; and how are you going to make millions of people of different quantities and qualities and amount of brain, clad in this living robe of passionate flesh, how are you going to make millions of them think alike ?

—From Copernicus we learned that this earth is only a grain of sand on the infinite shore of the universe; that everywhere we are surrounded by shining worlds vastly greater than our own, all moving and existing in accordance with law. True, the earth began to grow small, but man began to grow great.

—The last Napoleon was not satisfied with being the emperor of the French. He was not satisfied with having a circlet of gold about his head. He wanted some evidence that he had something of value within his head. So he wrote the life of Julius Cæsar that he might become a member of the French Academy.

—Abraham Lincoln was, in my judgment, in many respects, the grandest man ever President of the United States. Upon his monument these words should be written : "Here sleeps the only man in the history of the world who, having been clothed with almost absolute power, never abused it except upon the side of mercy."

—A government founded upon anything except liberty and justice cannot and ought not to stand. All the wrecks on either side of the stream of time, all the wrecks of the great cities, and all the nations that have passed away—all are a warning that no nation founded upon injustice can stand. From the sand-enshrouded Egypt, from the marble wilderness of Athens, and from every fallen, crumbling stone of the once mighty Rome, comes a wail, as it were, the cry that no nation founded upon injustice can permanently stand.

—I have some excuses to offer for the race to which I belong. My first excuse is that this is not a very good world to raise folks in anyway. It is not very well adapted to raising magnificent people. There's only a quarter of it land to start with. It is three times better fitted for raising fish than folks; and in that one-quarter of land there is not a tenth part fit to raise people on. You can't raise people without a good climate. You have got to have the right kind of climate, and you have got to have certain elements in the soil or you can't raise good people. Do you know that there is only a little zig zag strip around the world within which have been produced all men of genius ?

—In my judgment the black people have suffered enough. They have been slaves for two hundred years. They have been owned two hundred years, and, more than all, they have been compelled to keep the company of those who owned them. Think of being compelled to keep the society of a man who is stealing from you. Think of being compelled to live with a man that stole your child from the cradle before your very eyes. Think of being compelled to live with a thief all your life, to spend your days with a white loafer, and to be under his control. For two hundred years they were bought and sold and branded like cattle. For two hundred years every human tie was rent and torn asunder by the brutal, bloody hand of avarice.

and might; and for that reason I am in favor of this Government protecting them in every right they have got in every Southern State, if it takes another war to do it.

—It is often said of this or that man that he is a self-made man—that he was born of the poorest and humblest parents, and that with every obstacle to overcome he became great. This is a mistake. Poverty is generally an advantage. Most of the intellectual giants of the world have been nursed at the sad but loving breast of poverty. Most of those who have climbed highest on the shining ladder of fame commenced at the lowest round. They were reared in the straw thatched cottages of Europe; in the log houses of America; in the factories of the great cities; in the midst of toil; in the smoke and din of labor, and on the verge of want. They were rocked by the feet of mothers whose hands, at the same time, were busy with the needle or the wheel.

—The superior man is the man who helps his fellow-men; the superior man is the useful man; the superior man is the kind man, the man who lifts up his down-trodden brothers; and the greater load of human sorrow and human want you can get in your arms the higher you can climb the great hill of fame. The superior man is the man who loves his fellow-men. Let me say right here, the superior men, the grand men, are brothers the world over. No matter what their complexion—continents may divide them—yet they embrace each other. Centuries may separate, yet they are hand in hand, and all the good and all the grand and all the superior men, shoulder to shoulder, heart to heart, are fighting the great battle for the progress of mankind.

—All the advance that has been made in the science of medicine has been made by the recklessness of patients. I can recollect when they wouldn't give a man water in a fever—not a drop. Now and then some fellow would get so thirsty he would say: "Well, I'll die anyway, so I'll drink it," and thereupon he would drink a gallon of water, and thereupon he would burst into a generous perspiration and get well, and the next morning when the doctor would come to see him they would tell him about the man drinking the water, and he would say: "How much?"

"Well, he swallowed two pitchers full."

"Is he alive?" "Yes."

So they would go into the room and the doctor would feel his pulse and ask him:

"Did you drink two pitchers of water?"

"Yes."

"My God! what a constitution you have got."

—I think we came from the lower animals. I am not dead sure of it, but think so. When I first read about it I didn't like it. My heart was filled with sympathy for those people who leave nothing to be proud of except ancestors. I thought how terrible this will be upon the nobility of the old world. Think of their being forced to trace their ancestry back to the Duke Orang-Outang or to the Princess Chimpanzee. After thinking it all over I came to the conclusion that I liked that doctrine. I became convinced in spite of myself. I read about rudimentary bones and muscles. I was told that everybody had rudimentary muscles extending from the ear into the cheek. I asked: "What are they?" I was told: "They are the remains of muscles; they became rudimentary from the lack of use." They went into bankruptcy. They are the muscles with which your ancestors used to flap their ears. Well, at first I was greatly astonished, and afterward I was more astonished to find they had become rudimentary.

Part II.
GREAT SPEECHES.

COL. INGERSOLL'S
THREE GREAT SPEECHES.

I.—TO THE FARMERS ON FARMING.

INGERSOLL'S EARLY EXPERIENCE WHEN HE WAS A FARMER—
A RETROSPECTIVE VIEW.

[*From the Illinois State Register.*]

LADIES AND GENTLEMEN: I am not an old and experienced farmer, nor a tiller of the soil, nor one of the hard-handed sons of labor. I imagine, however, that I know something about cultivating the soil, and getting happiness out of the ground.

I know enough to know that agriculture is the basis of all wealth, prosperity and luxury. I know that in the country where the tillers of the fields are free, everybody is free and ought to be prosperous.

The old way of farming was a great mistake. Everything was done the wrong way. It was all work and waste, weariness and want. They used to fence a hundred and sixty acres of land with a couple of dogs. Everything was left to the protection of the blessed trinity of chance, accident and mistake.

When I was a farmer they used to haul wheat two hun-

3

dred miles in wagons and sell it for thirty-five cents a bushel. They would bring home about three hundred feet of lumber, two bunches of shingles, a barrel of salt, and a cook-stove that never would draw and never did bake.

In those blessed days the people lived on corn and bacon. Cooking was an unknown art. Eating was a necessity, not a pleasure. It was hard work for the cook to keep on good terms even with hunger.

We had poor houses. The rain held the roofs in perfect contempt, and the snow drifted joyfully on the floors and beds. They had no barns. The horses were kept in rail pens surrounded with straw. Long before spring the sides would be eaten away and nothing but roofs would be left. Food is fuel. When the cattle were exposed to all the blasts of winter, it took all the corn and oats that could be stuffed into them to prevent actual starvation.

In those times farmers thought the best place for the pig-pen was immediately in front of the house. There is nothing like sociability.

Women were supposed to know the art of making fires without fuel. The wood-pile consisted, as a general thing, of one log, upon which an axe or two had been worn out in vain. There was nothing to kindle a fire with. Pickets were pulled from the garden fence, clap-boards taken from the house, and every stray plank was seized upon for kindling. Everything was done in the hardest way. Everything about the farm was disagreeable. Nothing was kept in order. Nothing was preserved. The wagons stood in the sun and rain, and the plows rusted in the fields. There was no leisure, no feeling that the work was done. It was all labor and weariness and vexation of spirit. The crops were destroyed by wandering herds, or they were put in too late, or too early, or they were blown down, or caught by the frost, or devoured by bugs, or stung by flies, or

eaten by worms, or carried away by birds, or dug up by
gophers, or washed away by floods, or dried up by the sun,
or rotted in the stack, or heated in the crib, or they all run
to vines, or tops, or straw, or smut, or cobs. And when
in spite of all these accidents that lie in wait between the
plow and the reaper, they did succeed in raising a good
crop and a high price was offered, then the roads would be
impassable. And when the roads got good, then the prices
went down. Everything worked together for evil.

Nearly every farmer's boy took an oath that he would
never cultivate the soil. The moment they arrived at the
age of twenty-one they left the desolate and dreary farms
and rushed to the towns and cities. They wanted to be
book-keepers, doctors, merchants, railroad men, insurance
agents, lawyers, even preachers, anything to avoid the
drudgery of the farm. Nearly every boy acquainted with
the three R's—reading, writing and arithmetic—imagined
that he had altogether more education than ought to be
wasted in raising potatoes and corn. They made haste to
get into some other business. Those who stayed upon the
farm envied those who went away.

A few years ago the times were prosperous, and the young
men went to the cities to enjoy the fortunes that were
waiting for them. They wanted to engage in something
that promised quick returns. They built railways, established banks and insurance companies. They speculated
in stocks in Wall street, and gambled in grain at Chicago.
They became rich. They lived in palaces. They rode in
carriages. They pitied their poor brothers on the farms,
and the poor brothers envied them.

But time has brought its revenge. The farmers have
seen the railroad president a bankrupt, and the road in the
hands of a receiver. They have seen the bank president
abscond, and the insurance company a wrecked and ruined

fraud. The only solvent people, as a class, the only inde
pendent people, are the tillers of the soil.

Farming must be made more attractive. The comforts
of the town must be added to the beauty of the fields. The
sociability of the city must be rendered possible in the
country.

Farming has been made repulsive. The farmers have
been unsociable, and their homes have been lonely. They
have been wasteful and careless. They have not been
proud of their business.

No farmer can afford to raise corn and oats and hay to
sell. He should sell horses, not oats; sheep, cattle and
pork, not corn. He should make every profit possible out
of what he produces. So long as the farmers of the Middle
States ship their corn and oats, so long they will be poor,—
just so long will their farms be mortgaged to the insurance
companies and banks of the east,—just so long will they do
the work, and others reap the benefit,—just so long will
they be poor, and the money lenders grow rich,—just so
long will cunning avarice grasp and hold the net profits of
honest toil. When the farmers of the west ship beef and
pork instead of grain,—when we manufacture here,—when
we cease paying tribute to others, ours will be the most
prosperous country in the world.

Another thing—It is just as cheap to raise a good as a
poor breed of cattle. Scrubs will eat just as much as
thoroughbreds. If you are not able to buy Durhams and
Alderneys, you can raise the corn-breed. By "corn-breed"
I mean the cattle that have for several generations had
enough to eat, and have been treated with kindness. Every
farmer who will treat his cattle kindly, and feed them all
they want, will, in a few years, have blooded stock on his

farm. All blooded stock has been produced in this way. You can raise good cattle just as you can raise good people. If you wish to raise a good boy you must give him plenty to eat, and treat him with kindness. In this way, and in this way only, can good cattle or good people be produced.

Another thing—You must beautify your homes.

When I was a farmer it was not fashionable to set out trees, nor to plant vines.

When you visited the farm you were not welcomed by flowers, and greeted by trees loaded with fruit. Yellow dogs came bounding over the tumbled fence like wild beasts. There is no sense—there is no profit in such a life. It is not living. The farmers ought to beautify their homes. There should be trees and grass, and flowers and running vines. Everything should be kept in order; gates should be kept on their hinges, and about all there snould be the pleasant air of thrift. In every house there should be a bath-room. The bath is a civilizer, a refiner, a beautifier. When you come from the fields tired, covered with dust, nothing is so refreshing. Above all things, keep clean. It is not necessary to be a pig in order to raise one. In the cool of the evening, after a day in the field, put on clean clothes, take a seat under the trees, 'mid the perfume of flowers, surrounded by your family, and you will know what it is to enjoy life like a gentleman.

WHAT THE COLONEL BELIEVES TO BE THE BEST PORTION OF THE EARTH.

In no part of the globe will farming pay better than in the Western States You are in the best portion of the earth. From the Atlantic to the Pacific, there is no such country as yours. The east is hard and stony ; the soil is stingy. The far west is a desert parched and barren, dreary and desolate as perdition would be with the fires out. It

is better to dig wheat and corn from the soil than gold.
Only a few days ago I was where they wrench the precious
metals from the miserly clutch of the rocks. When I saw
the mountains, treeless, shrubless, flowerless, without even
a spire of grass, it seemed to me that gold had the same
effect upon the country that holds it, as upon the man who
lives and labors only for that. It affects the land as it does
the man. It leaves the heart barren without a flower of
kindness—without a blossom of pity.

The farmer in the Middle States has the best soil—the
greatest return for the least labor—more leisure—more
time for enjoyment than any other farmer in the world.
His hard work ceases with autumn. He has the long win-
ters in which to become acquainted with his family—with
his neighbors—-in which to read and keep abreast with the
advanced thought of his day. He has the time and means
of self-culture. He has more time than the mechanic, the
merchant or the professional man. If the farmer is not
well informed it is his own fault. Books are cheap, and
every farmer can have enough to give him the outline of
every science, and an idea of all that has been accomplished
by man.

THE FARMER AND THE MECHANIC—WHICH THE COLONEL THINKS
HAS THE BEST OF IT.

In many respects the farmer has the advantage of the
mechanic. In our time we have plenty of mechanics but
no tradesmen. In the sub-division of labor we have a
thousand men working upon different parts of the same
thing, each taught in one particular branch, and in only
one. We have, say, in a shoe-factory, hundreds of men,
but not a shoemaker. It takes them all, assisted by a great
number of machines, to make a shoe. Each does a particular part, and not one of them knows the entire trade.

The result is that the moment the factory shuts down these men are out of employment. Out of employment means out of bread—out of bread means famine and horror. The mechanic of to-day has but little independence. His prosperity often depends upon the good-will of one man. He is liable to be discharged for a look, for a word. He lays by but little for his declining years. He is, at the best, the slave of capital.

It is a thousand times better to be a whole farmer than part of a mechanic. It is better to till the ground and work for yourself than to be hired by corporations. Every man should endeavor to belong to himself.

About seven hundred years ago, Kheyam, a Persian, said: "Why should a man who possesses a piece of bread securing life for two days, and who has a cup of water— why should such a man serve another?"

Young men should not be satisfied with a salary. Do not mortgage the possibilities of your future. Have the courage to take life as it comes, feast or famine. Think of hunting a gold mine for a dollar a day, and think of finding one for another man. How would you feel then?

We are lacking in true courage, when, for fear of the future, we take the crusts and scraps and niggardly salaries of the present. I had a thousand times rather have a farm and be independent, than to be President of the United States without independence, filled with doubt and trembling, feeling of the popular pulse, resorting to art and artifice, inquiring about the wind of opinion, and succeeding at last in losing my self-respect without gaining the respect of others.

Man needs more manliness, more real independence. We must take care of ourselves. This we can do by labor, and in this way we can preserve our independence. We should try and choose that business or profession the pursuit of which will give us the most happiness. Happiness is wealth. We can be happy without being rich—without holding office—without being famous. I am not sure that we can be happy with wealth, with office, or with fame.

THE FARMER AND THE PROFESSIONAL MAN—THE RACE OF LIFE.

There is a quiet about the life of a farmer, and the hope of a serene old age, that no other business or profession can promise. A professional man is doomed some time to feel that his powers are waning. He is doomed to see younger and stronger men pass him in the race of life. He looks forward to an old age of intellectual mediocrity. He will be last where once he was the first. But the farmer goes, as it were, into partnership with nature—he lives with trees and flowers—he breathes the sweet air of the fields. There is no constant and frightful strain upon his mind. His nights are filled with sleep and rest. He watches his flocks and herds as they feed upon the green and sunny slopes. He hears the pleasant rain falling upon the waving corn, and the trees he planted in youth rustle above him as he plants others for the children yet to be.

Our country is filled with the idle and unemployed, and the great question asking for an answer is: What shall be done with these men? What shall these men do? To this there is but one answer: They must cultivate the soil.

COL. INGERSOLL'S IDEA OF AN EDUCATED FARMER.

Farming must be more attractive. Those who work the land must have an honest pride in their business. They must educate their children to cultivate the soil. They must make farming easier, so that their children will not hate it themselves. The boys must not be taught that

tilling the soil is a curse and almost a disgrace. They
must not suppose that education is thrown away upon them
unless they become ministers, lawyers, doctors or statesmen. It must be understood that education can be used
to advantage on a farm. We must get rid of the idea that
a little learning unfits one for work. There are hundreds
of graduates of Yale and Harvard and other colleges, who
are agents of sewing machines, solicitors for insurance,
clerks, copyists, in short, performing a hundred varieties of
menial service. They seem willing to do anything that is
not regarded as work—anything that can be done in a town,
in the house, in an office, but they avoid farming as they
would a leprosy. Nearly every young man educated in
this way is simply ruined. 'Such an education ought to be
called ignorance. It is a thousand times better to have
common-sense without education, than education without
the sense. Boys and girls should be educated to help
themselves. They should be taught that it is disgraceful
to be idle, and dishonorable to be useless.

I say again, if you want more men and women on the
farms, something must be done to make farm-life pleasant.
One great difficulty is that the farm is lonely. People
write about the pleasures of solitude, but they are found
only in books. He who lives long alone becomes insane.
A hermit is a mad man. Without friends and wife and
child, there is nothing left worth living for. The unsocial
are the enemies of joy. They are filled with egotism and
envy, with vanity and hatred. People who live much
alone become narrow and suspicious. They are apt to be
the property of one idea. They begin to think there is no
use in anything. They look upon the happiness of others
as a kind of folly. They hate joyous folks, because, way
down in their hearts, they envy them.

In our country farm-life is too lonely. The farms are large, and neighbors are too far apart. In these days, when the roads are filled with "tramps," the wives and children need protection. When the farmer leaves home and goes to some distant field to work, a shadow of fear is upon his heart all day, and a like shadow rests upon all at home.

In the early settlement of our country the pioneer was forced to take his family, his axe, his dog and his gun, and go into the far wild forest, and build his cabin miles and miles from any neighbor. He saw the smoke from his hearth go up alone in all the wide and lonely sky.

But this necessity has passed away, and now, instead of living so far apart upon the lonely farms, you should live in villages. With the improved machinery which you have —with your generous soil—with your markets and means of transportation, you can now afford to live together.

You should live in villages, so that you can have the benefits of social life. You can have a reading-room—you can take the best papers and magazines—you can have plenty of books, and each one can have the benefit of them all. Some of the young men and women can cultivate music. You can have social gatherings—you can learn from each other—you can discuss all topics of interest, and in this way you can make farming a delightful business. You must keep up with the age. The way to make farming respectable is for farmers to become really intelligent. They must live intelligent and happy lives. They must not be satisfied with knowing something of the affairs of a neighborhood and nothing about the rest of the earth. The business must be made attractive, and it never can be until the farmer has prosperity, intelligence and leisure.

THE COLONEL'S AMUSING REMARKS ABOUT GETTING UP EARLY
IN THE MORNING.

It is not necessary in this age of the world for the farmer to rise in the middle of the night and begin his work. This getting up so early in the morning is a relic of barbarism. It has made hundreds of thousands of young men curse the business. There is no need of getting up at three or four o'clock in the winter morning. The farmer who persists in dragging his wife and children from their beds ought to be visited by a missionary. It is time enough to rise after the sun has set the example. For what purpose do you get up? To feed the cattle? Why not feed them more the night before? It is a waste of life. In the old times they used to get up about three o'clock in the morning, and go to work long before the sun had risen with "healing upon his wings," and as a just punishment they all had the ague; and they ought to have it now. The man who cannot get a living upon Illinois soil without rising before daylight ought to starve. Eight hours a day is enough for any farmer to work except in harvest time. When you rise at four and work till dark what is life worth? Of what use are all the improvements in farming? Of what use is all the improved machinery unless it tends to give the farmer a little more leisure? What is harvesting now, compared with what is was in the old time? Think of the days of reaping, of cradling, of raking and binding and mowing. Think of threshing with the flail and winnowing with the wind. And now think of the reapers and mowers, the binders and threshing machines, the plows and cultivators, upon which the farmer rides protected from the sun. If, with all these advantages, you cannot get a living without rising in the middle of the night, go into some other business. You should not rob your families of sleep.

Sleep is the best medicine in the world. There is no such thing as health without plenty of sleep. Sleep until you are thoroughly rested and restored. When you work, work; and when you get through take a good, long and refreshing sleep.

THE FASHIONS AND HANDSOME WOMEN.

Another thing—I am a believer in fashion. It is the duty of every woman to make herself as beautiful and attractive as she possibly can.

"Handsome is as handsome does," but she is much handsomer if well dressed. Every man should look his very best. I am a believer in good clothes. The time never ought to come in this country when you can tell a farmer's wife or daughter simply by the garments she wears. I say to every girl and woman, no matter what the material of your dress may be, no matter how cheap and coarse it is, cut it and make it in the fashion. I believe in jewelry. Some people look upon it as barbaric, but in my judgment, wearing jewelry is the first evidence the barbarian gives of a wish to be civilized. To adorn ourselves seems to be a part of our nature, and this desire seems to be everywhere and in everything. I have sometimes thought that the desire for beauty covers the earth with flowers. It is this desire that paints the wings of moths, tints the chamber of the shell, and gives the bird its plumage and its song. Oh! daughters and wives, if you would be loved, adorn yourselves—if you would be adored, be beautiful!

HOME *vs.* THE BOARDING-HOUSE.

There is another fault common with the farmers of our country—they want too much land. You cannot, at present, when taxes are high, afford to own land that you do not cultivate. Sell it and let others make farms and homes.

In this way what you keep will be enhanced in value. Farmers ought to own the land they cultivate, and cultivate what they own. Renters can hardly be called farmers. There can be no such thing in the highest sense as a home unless you own it. There must be an incentive to plant trees, to beautify the grounds, to preserve and improve. It elevates a man to own a home. It gives a certain independence, a force of character that is obtained in no other way. A man without a home feels like a passenger. There is in such a man a little of the vagrant. Homes make patriots. He who has sat by his own fireside with wife and children, will defend it. When he hears the word country pronounced, he thinks of his home.

Few men have been patriotic enough to shoulder a musket in defense of a boarding house.

The prosperity and glory of our country depend upon the number of our people who are the owners of homes. Around the fireside cluster the private and the public virtues of our race. Raise your sons to be independent through labor—to pursue some business for themselves, and upon their own account—to be self-reliant—to act upon their own responsibility, and to take the consequences like men. Teach them above all things to be good, true and faithful husbands—winners of love, and builders of homes.

INDUSTRY AND BROTHERHOOD.

A great many farmers seem to think that they are the only laborers in the world. This is a very foolish thing. Farmers cannot get along without the mechanic. You are not independent of the man of genius. Your prosperity depends upon the inventor. The world advances by the assistance of all laborers; and all labor is under obligations to the inventions of genius. The inventor does as much for agriculture as he who tills the soil. All laboring men should be brothers. You are in partnership with the mechanics who make your reapers, your mowers and your plows; and you should take into your granges all the men who make their living by honest labor. The laboring people should unite and should protect themselves against all idlers. You can divide mankind into two classes: the laborers and the idlers, the supporters and the supported, the honest and the dishonest. Every man is dishonest who lives upon the unpaid labor of others, no matter if he occupies a throne. All laborers should be brothers. The laborers should have equal rights before the world and before the law. And I want every farmer to consider every man who labors either with hand or brain as his brother. Until genius and labor formed a partnership there was no such thing as prosperity among men. Every reaper and mower, every agricultural implement, has elevated the work of the farmer, and his vocation grows grander with every invention. In the olden time the agriculturist was ignorant; he knew nothing of machinery, he was the slave of superstition.

The farmer has been elevated through science, and he should not forget the debt he owes to the mechanic, to the inventor, to the thinker. He should remember that all laborers belong to the same grand family—that they are the real kings and queens, the only true nobility.

WHAT THE RAILROADS HAVE DONE—THIRTY-THREE DOZEN EGGS FOR ONE DOLLAR.

Another idea entertained by most farmers is that they are in some mysterious way oppressed by every other kind of business—that they are devoured by monopolies, especially by railroads.

Of course, the railroads are indebted to the farmers for their prosperity, and the farmers are indebted to the railroads.

A few years ago you endeavored to regulate the charges of railroad companies. The principal complaint you had was that they charged too much for the transportation of corn and other cereals to the East. You should remember that all freight are paid by the consumers of the grain. You are really interested in transportation from the East to the West and in local freights. The result is that while you have put down through freights you have not succeeded so well in local freights. The exact opposite should be the policy in Illinois. Put down local freights; put them down, if you can, to the lowest possible figure, and let through freights take care of themselves. If all the corn raised in Illinois could be transported to New York absolutely free, it would enhance but little the price that you would receive. What we want is the lowest possible local rate. Instead of this you have simply succeeded in helping the East at the expense of the West. The railroads are your friends. They are your partners. They can prosper only where the country through which they run prospers. All intelligent railroad men know this. They know that present robbery is future bankruptcy. They know that the interest of the farmer and of the railroad is the same. We must have railroads. What can we do without them?

When we had no railroads, we drew, as I said before, our grain two hundred miles to market.

In those days the farmers did not stop at hotels. They slept under the wagons—took with them their food—fried their own bacon, made their own coffee, and ate their meals in the snow and rain. Those were the days when they received ten cents a bushels for corn—when they sold four bushels of potatoes for a quarter—thirty-three dozen eggs for a dollar, and a hundred pounds of pork for a dollar and a half.

What has made the difference? The railroads came to

your door and they brought with them the markets of the world. They brought New York and Liverpool and London into Illinois, and the State has been clothed with prosperity as with a mantle. It is the interest of the farmer to protect every great interest in the State. In these iron highways more than three hundred million dollars have been invested—a sum equal to ten times the original cost of all the land in the State. To make war upon the railroads is a short-sighted and suicidal policy. They should be treated fairly and should be taxed by the same standard that farms are taxed, and in no other way. If we wish to prosper we must act together, and we must see to it that every form of labor is protected.

BUSINESS AND THE MONEY QUESTION.

There has been a long period of depression in all business. The farmers have suffered least of all. Your land is just as rich and productive as ever. Prices have been reasonable. The towns and cities have suffered. Stocks and bonds have shrunk from par to worthless paper. Princes have become paupers, and bankers, merchants and millionaires have passed into the oblivion of bankruptcy. The period of depression is slowly passing away, and we are entering upon better times.

A great many people say that a scarcity of money is our only difficulty. In my opinion we have money enough, but we lack confidence in each other in the future.

There has been so much dishonesty, there have been so many failures, that the people are afraid to trust anybody. There is plenty of money, but there seems to be a scarcity of business. If you were to go to the owner of a ferry, and, upon seeing his boat lying high and dry on the shore, should say, "There is a superabundance of ferry-boat," he would probably reply, "No, but there is a scarcity of water.'' So with us there is not a scarcity f money, but there is a scarcity of business. And this scarcity springs from lack of confidence in one another. So many presidents of savings banks, even those belonging to the Young Men's Christian Association, run off with the funds; so many railroad and insurance companies are in the hands of receivers; there is so much bankruptcy on every hand, that all capital is held in the nervous clutch of fear. Slowly, but surely, we are coming back to honest methods in business. Confidence will return, and then enterprise will unlock the safe and money will again circulate as of yore; the dollars will leave their hiding places, and every one will be seeking investment.

For my part I do not ask any interference on the part of the government except to undo the wrong it has done. I do not ask that money be made out of nothing. I do not ask for the prosperity born of paper. But I do ask for the remonetization of silver. Silver was demonetized by fraud. It was an imposition upon every solvent man; a fraud upon every honest debtor in the United States. It assassinated labor. It was done in the interest of avarice and greed, and should be undone by honest men.

The farmers should vote only for such men as are able and willing to guard and advance the interests of labor. We should know better than to vote for men who will deliberately put a tariff of three dollars a thousand upon Canada lumber, when every farmer in the States is a purchaser of lumber. People who live upon the prairies ought to vote for cheap lumber. We should protect ourselves. We ought to have intelligence enough to know what we want and how to get it. The real laboring men of this country can succeed if they are united. By laboring men, I do not mean only the farmers. I mean all who contribute in some way to the general welfare. They should forget prejudices and party names, and remember only the best interests of the people. Let us see if we cannot protect every department of industry. Let us see if all property cannot be protected alike and taxed alike, whether owned by individuals or corporations.

Where industry creates and justice protects, prosperity dwells.

ILLINOIS.

Let me tell you something about Illinois. We have fifty-six thousand square miles of land—nearly thirty-six million acres. Upon these plains we can raise enough to feed and clothe twenty million people. Beneath these prairies were hidden, millions of ages ago, by that old miser, the sun, thirty-six thousand square miles of coal. The aggregate thickness of these veins is at least fifteen feet. Think of a column of coal one mile square and one hundred miles high! All this came from the sun. What a sunbeam such a column would be! Think of all this force, willed and left to us by the dead morning of the world! Think of the fireside of the future around which will sit the fathers, mothers and children of the years to be! Think of the sweet and happy faces, the loving and tender eyes that will glow and gleam in the sacred light of all these flames!

We have the best country in the world. Is there any reason that our farmers should not be prosperous and happy men? They have every advantage, and within their reach are all the comforts and conveniences of life.

Do not get the land fever and think you must buy all the land that joins you. Get out of debt as soon as you possibly can. A mortgage casts a shadow on the sunniest field. There is no business under the sun that can pay ten per cent.

WHAT A DOLLAR CAN DO.

Ainsworth R. Spofford gives the following facts about

interest: "One dollar loaned for one hundred years at six per cent., with the interest collected annually and added to the principal, will amount to three hundred and forty dollars. At eight per cent. it amounts to two thousand two hundred and three dollars. At three per cent. it amounts only to nineteen dollars and twenty-five cents. At ten per cent. it is thirteen thousand eight hundred and nine dollars, or about seven hundred times as much. At twelve per cent. it amounts to eighty-four thousand and seventy-five dollars, or more than four thousand times as much. At eighteen per cent. it amounts to fifteen million one hundred and forty-five thousand and seven dollars. At twenty-four per cent. (which we sometimes hear talked of) it reaches the enormous sum of two billion five hundred and fifty-one million seven hundred and ninety-nine thousand four hundred and four dollars."

One dollar at compound interest, at twenty-four per cent., for one hundred years, would produce a sum equal to our national debt.

Interest eats night and day, and the more it eats the hungrier it grows. The farmer in debt, lying awake at night, can, if he listens, hear it gnaw. If he owes nothing, he can hear his corn grow. Get out of debt as soon as you possibly can. You have supported idle avarice and lazy economy long enough.

HOW A MAN SHOULD TREAT HIS WIFE AND CHILDREN.

Above all, let every farmer treat his wife and children with infinite kindness. Give your sons and daughters every advantage within your power. In the air of kindness they will grow about you like flowers. They will fill your homes with sunshine and all your years with joy. Do not try to rule by force. A blow from a parent leaves a scar on the soul. I should feel ashamed to die surrounded by children

I had whipped. Think of feeling upon your dying lips the kiss of a child you had struck.

See to it that your wife has every convenience. Make her life worth living. Never allow her to become a servant. Wives, weary and worn; mothers, wrinkled and bent before their time, fill homes with grief and shame. If you are not able to hire help for your wives, help them yourselves. See that they have the best utensils to work with. Women cannot create things by magic. Have plenty of wood and coal—good cellars and plenty in them. Have cisterns, so that you can have plenty of rain water for washing. Do not rely on a barrel and a board. When the rain comes the board will be lost or the hoops will be off the barrel.

Farmers should live like princes. Eat the best things you raise and sell the rest. Have good things to cook and good things to cook with. Of all people in our country, you should live the best. Throw your miserable little stoves out of the window. Get ranges, and have them so built that your wife need not burn her face off to get you a breakfast. Do not make her cook in a kitchen hot as the orthodox perdition. The beef, not the cook, should be roasted. It is just as easy to have things convenient and right as to have them any other way.

INGERSOLL ON COOKERY.

Cooking is one of the fine arts. Give your wives and daughters things to cook, and things to cook with, and they will soon become most excellent cooks. Good cooking is the basis of civilization. The man whose arteries and veins are filled with rich blood made of good and well-cooked food, has pluck, courage, endurance and noble impulses. Remember that your wife should have things to cook with.

In the good old days there would be eleven children in

the family and only one skillet. Everything was broken
or cracked or loaned or lost.

There ought to be a law making it a crime, punishable
by imprisonment, to fry beefsteak. Broil it; it is just as
easy, and when broiled it is delicious. Fried beefsteak is
not fit for a wild beast. You can broil even on a stove.
Shut the front damper—open the back one, then take off a
griddle. There will then be a draft downwards through
this opening. Put on your steak, using a wire broiler, and
not a particle of smoke will touch it, for the reason that the
smoke goes down. If you try to broil it with the front
damper open, the smoke will rise. For broiling, coal, even
soft coal, makes a better fire than wood.

There is no reason why farmers should not have fresh
meat all the year round. There is certainly no sense in
stuffing yourself full of salt meat every morning, and making
a well or a cistern of your stomach for the rest of the day.
Every farmer should have an ice house. Upon or near
every farm is some stream from which plenty of ice can be
obtained, and the long summer days made delightful. Dr.
Draper, one of the world's greatest scientists, says that ice
water is healthy, and that it has done away with many of
the low forms of fever in the great cities. Ice has become
one of the necessaries of civilized life, and without it there
is very little comfort.

THE HAPPY HOME.

Make your homes pleasant. Have your houses warm
and comfortable for the winter. Do not build a story-and-
a-half house. The half-story is simply an oven in which,
during the summer, you will bake every night, and feel in
the morning as though only the rind of yourself was left.

Decorate your rooms, even if you do so with cheap
engravings. The cheapest are far better than none. Have
books—have papers, and read them. You have more

leisure than the dwellers in cities. Beautify your grounds with plants and flowers and vines. Have good gardens. Remember that everything of beauty tends to the elevation of man. Every little morning-glory whose purple bosom is thrilled with the amorous kisses of the sun, tends to put a blossom in your heart. Do not judge of the value of everything by the market reports. Every flower about a house certifies to the refinement of somebody. Every vine, climbing and blossoming, tells of love and joy.

Make your houses comfortable. Do not huddle together in a little room around a red-hot stove, with every window fastened down. Do not live in this poisoned atmosphere, and then, when one of your children dies, put a piece in the papers commencing with, "Whereas, it has pleased divine Providence to remove from our midst—." Have plenty of air, and plenty of warmth. Comfort is health. Do not imagine anything is unhealthy simply because it is pleasant. This is an old and foolish idea.

Let your children sleep. Do not drag them from their beds in the darkness of night. Do not compel them to associate all that is tiresome, irksome and dreadful with cultivating the soil. In this way you bring farming into hatred and disrepute. Treat your children with infinite kindness—treat them as equals. There is no happiness in a home not filled with love. Where the husband hates his wife—where the wife hates the husband; where children hate their parents and each other—there is a hell upon earth.

There is no reason why farmers should not be the kindest and most cultivated of men. There is nothing in plowing the fields to make men cross, cruel and crabbed. To look upon the sunny slopes covered with daisies does not tend to make men unjust. Whoever labors for the happiness of those he loves, elevates himself, no matter whether he works in the dark and dreary shops, or in the perfumed fields. To work for others is, in reality, the only way in which a man can work for himself. Selfishness is ignorance. Speculators cannot make unless somebody loses. In the realm of speculation, every success has at least one victim. The harvest reaped by the farmer benefits all and injures none. For him to succeed, it is not necessary that some one should fail. The same is true of all producers—of all laborers.

THE COLONEL'S VIEW OF "SOLID COMFORT."

I can imagine no condition that carries with it such a promise of joy as that of the farmer in the early winter. He has his cellar filled—he has made every preparation for the days of snow and storm—he looks forward to three months of ease and rest; to three months of fireside content; three months with wife and children; three months of long, delightful evenings; three months of home; three months of solid comfort.

When the life of the farmer is such as I have described, the cities and towns will not be filled with want—the streets will not be crowded with wrecked rogues, broken bankers, and bankrupt speculators. The fields will be tilled, and country villages, almost hidden by trees, and vines, and flowers, filled with industrious and happy people, will nestle in every vale and gleam like gems on every plain.

The idea must be done away with that there is something intellectually degrading in cultivating the soil. Nothing can be noble than to be useful. Idleness should not be respectable.

If farmers will cultivate well, and without waste; if they will so build that their houses will be warm in winter and cool in summer; if they will plant trees and beautify their homes; if they will occupy their leisure in reading, in thinking, in improving their minds and in devising ways

and means to make their business profitable and pleasant;
if they will live nearer together and cultivate sociability;
if they will come together often; if they will have reading
rooms and cultivate music; if they will have bath-rooms,
ice-houses and good gardens; if their wives can have an
easy time; if the nights can be taken for sleep and the
evenings for enjoyment, everybody will be in love with the
fields. Happiness should be the object of life, and if life
on the farm can be made really happy, the children will
grow up in love with the meadows, the streams, the woods
and the old home. Around the farm will cling and cluster
the happy memories of the delightful years.

Remember, I pray you, that you are in partnership with
all labor---that you should join hands with all the sons and
daughters of toil, and that all who work belong to the same
noble family.

For my part, I envy the man who has lived on the same
broad acres from his boyhood, who cultivates the fields
where in youth he played, and lives where his father lived
and died.

I can imagine no sweeter way to end one's life than in
the quiet of the country, out of the mad race for money,
place and power—far from the demands of business—out
of the dusty highway where fools struggle and strive for
the hollow praise ot other fools.

Surrounded by these pleasant fields and faithful friends,
by those I have loved, I hope to end my days. And this I
hope may be the lot of all who hear my voice. I hope that
you, in the country, in houses covered with vines and
clothed with flowers, looking from the open window upon
rustling fields of corn and wheat, over which will run the
sunshine and the shadow, surrounded by those whose lives
you have filled with joy, will pass away serenely as the
Autumn dies.

II.—COL. INGERSOLL'S GREAT SPEECH TO THE VETERAN SOLDIERS.

DELIVERED AT INDIANAPOLIS.

REASONS WHY THE COLONEL IS NOT A DEMOCRAT.

[From the Indianapolis Journal.]

LADIES AND GENTLEMEN—FELLOW CITIZENS AND CITIZEN SOLDIERS: I am opposed to the Democratic party, and I will tell you why. Every State that seceded from the United States was a Democratic State. Every ordinance of secession that was drawn was drawn by a Democrat. Every man that endeavored to tear the old flag from the heaven that it enriches was a Democrat. Every man that tried to destroy this nation was a Democrat. Every enemy this great republic has had for twenty years has been a Democrat. Every man that shot Union soldiers was a Democrat. Every man that starved Union soldiers and refused them in the extremity of death, a crust, was a Democrat. Every man that loved slavery better than liberty was a Democrat. The man that assassinated Abraham Lincoln was a Democrat. Every man that sympathized with the assassin—every man glad that the noblest President ever elected was assassinated, was a Democrat. Every man that wanted the privilege of whipping another man to make him work for him for nothing and pay him with lashes on his naked back, was a Democrat. Every man that raised blood-hounds to pursue human beings was a Democrat. Every man that clutched from shrieking, shuddering, crouching mothers, babes from their breasts, and sold them into slavery, was a Democrat. Every man that impaired the credit of the United States, every man that swore we would never pay the bonds, every man that swore we would never redeem the greenbacks, every maligner of his country's credit, every calumniator of his country's honor, was a Democrat. Every man that resisted the draft, every man that hid in the bushes and shot at Union men simply because they were endeavoring to enforce the laws of their country, was a Democrat. Every man that wept over the corpse of slavery was a Democrat. Every man that cursed Lincoln because he issued the proclamation of emancipation —the grandest paper since the Declaration of Independence —every one of them was a Democrat. Every man that denounced the soldiers that bared their bosoms to the storms of shot and shell for the honor of America and for the sacred rights of man, was a Democrat. Every man that wanted an uprising in the North, that wanted to release the rebel prisoners that they might burn down the homes of Union soldiers above the heads of their wives and children, while the brave husbands, the heroic fathers, were in the front fighting for the honor of the old flag, every one of them was a Democrat. I am not through yet. Every man that believed this glorious nation of ours is a confederacy, every man that believed the old banner carried by our fathers through the Revolution, through the war of 1812, carried by our brothers over the plains of Mexico, carried by our brothers over the fields of the rebellion, simply stood for a contract, simply stood for an agreement, was a Democrat. Every man who believed that any State could go out of the Union at its pleasure, every man that believed the grand fabric of the American Government could be made to crumble instantly into dust at the touch of treason, was a Democrat. Every man that helped to burn orphan asylums in

New York, was a Democrat; every man that tried to fire the city of New York, although he knew that thousands would perish, and knew that the great serpents of flame leaping from buildings would clutch children from their mothers' arms—every wretch that did it was a Democrat. Recollect it! Every man that tried to spread small-pox and yellow fever in the North, as the instrumentalities of civilized war, was a Democrat. Soldiers, every scar you have got on your heroic bodies was given you by a Democrat. Every scar, every arm that is lacking, every limb that is gone, every scar is a souvenir of a Democrat. I want you to recollect it. Every man that was the enemy of human liberty in this country was a Democrat. Every man that wanted the fruit of all the heroism of all the ages to turn to ashes upon the lips—every one was a Democrat.

WHY THE COLONEL IS A REPUBLICAN.

I am a Republican. I will tell you why: This is the only free government in the world. The Republican party made it so. The Republican party took the chains from 4,000,000 of people. The Republican party, with the wand of progress, touched the auction-block and it became a school-house. The Republican party put down the rebellion, saved the nation, kept the old banner afloat in the air, and declared that slavery of every kind should be extirpated from the face of the continent. What more? I am a Republican because it is the only free party that ever existed. It is a party that has a platform as broad as humanity, a platform as broad as the human race, a party that says you shall have all the fruit of the labor of your hands, a party that says you may think for yourself; a party that says no chains for the hands, no fetters for the soul. (A voice—"Amen." Cheers.) At this point the rain began to descend, and it looked as if a heavy shower

was impending. Several umbrellas were put up. Gov.
Noyes—"God bless you! What is rain to soldiers?"
Voice—"Go ahead; we don't mind the rain." (It was
proposed to adjourn the meeting to Masonic Hall, but the
motion was voted down by an overwhelming majority, and
Mr. Ingersoll proceeded.) I am a Republican because the
Republican party says this country is a nation, and not a
confederacy. I am here in Indiana to speak, and I have
as good a right to speak here in Indiana as though I had
been born on this stand—not because the State flag of Indiana waves over me. I would not know it if I should see
it. You have the same right to speak in Illinois, not because the State flag of Illinois waves over you, but because
that banner, rendered sacred by the blood of all the heroes,
waves over me and you. I am in favor of this being a nation. Think of a man gratifying his entire ambition in the
State of Rhode Island. We want this to be a nation, and
you can't have a great, grand, splendid people without a
great, grand, splendid country. The great plains, the
sublime mountains, the great rushing, roaring rivers, shores
lashed by two oceans, and the grand anthem of Niagara,
mingle and enter, as it were, in the character of every
American citizen, and make him or tend to make him a
great and a grand character. I am for the Republican
party because it says the government has as much right,
as much power to protect its citizens at home as abroad.
The Republican party don't say you have to go away from
home to get the protection of the government. The Democratic party says the government can't march its troops
into the South to protect the rights of the citizens. It is a
lie. The government claims the right, and it is conceded
that the government has the right, to go to your house,
while you are sitting by your fireside with your wife and
children about you, and the old lady knitting, and the cat

playing with the yarn, and everybody happy and sweet—
the government claims the right to go to your fireside and
take you by force and put you into the army: take you
down to the valley and the shadow of hell, set you by the
ruddy, roaring guns, and make you fight for your flag.
Now, that being so, when the war is over and your country
is victorious, and you go back to your home, and a lot of
Democrats want to trample upon your rights, I want to
know if the government that took you from your fireside
and made you fight for it, I want to know if it is not bound
to fight for you. The flag that will not protect its protectors is a dirty rag that contaminates the air in which it
waves. The government that will not defend its defenders
is a disgrace to the nations of the world. I am a Republican because the Republican party says, "We will protect
the rights of American citizens at home, and if necessary
we will march an army into any State to protect the rights
of the humblest American citizen in that State." I am a
Republican because that party allows me to be free—allows
me to do my own thinking in my own way. I am a Republican because it is a party grand enough and splendid
enough and sublime enough to invite every human being
in favor of liberty and progress to fight shoulder to shoulder for the advancement of mankind. It invites the Meth-
odist; it invites the Catholic; it invites the Presbyterian
and every kind of sectarian; it invites the free-thinker; it
invites the infidel. provided he is in favor of giving to every
other human being every chance and every right that he
claims for himself. I am a Republican, I tell you. There
is room in the Republican air for every wing; there is
room on the Republican sea for every sail. Republicanism
says to every man : " Let your soul be like an eagle; fly
out in the great dome of thought, and question the stars
for yourself." But the Democratic party says : " Be blind

owls; sit on the dry limb of a dead tree, and only hoot when Tilden & Co. tell you to."

In the Republican party there are no followers. We are all leaders. There is not a party chain. There is not a party lash. Any man that does not love this country, any man that does not love liberty, any man that is not in favor of human progress, that is not in favor of giving to others all he claims for himself; we don't ask him to vote the Republican ticket. You can vote it if you please, and if there is any Democrat within hearing who expects to die before another election, we are willing that he should vote one Republican ticket, simply as a consolation upon his death-bed. What more? I am a Republican because that party believes in free labor. It believes that free labor will give us wealth. It believes in free thought, because it believes that free thought will give us truth. You don't know what a grand party you belong to. I never want any holier or grander title of nobility than that I belong to the Republican party and have fought for the liberty of man. The Republican party, I say, believes in free labor. The Republican party also believes in slavery. What kind of slavery? In enslaving the forces of nature.

We believe that free labor, that free thought, have en-slaved the forces of nature, and made them work for man. We make old attraction of gravitation work for us; we make the lightning do our errands; we make steam ham-mer and fashion what we need. The forces of nature are the slaves of the Republican party. They have got no backs to be whipped; they have got no hearts to be torn—no hearts to be broken; they cannot be separated from their wives; they cannot be dragged from the bosoms of their husbands; they wo k night and day and they cannot tire. You cannot whip them, you cannot starve them, and a Democrat even can be trusted with one of them. I tell you I am a Republican. I believe, as I told you, that free labor will give us these slaves. Free labor will produce all these things, and everything you have got to-day has been produced by free labor, nothing by slave labor.

Slavery never invented but one machine, and that was a threshing-machine in the shape of a whip. Free labor has invented all the machines. We want to come down to the philosophy of these things. The problem of free labor, when a man works for the wife he loves, when he works for the little children he adores—the problem is to do the most work in the shortest space of time. The problem of slavery is to do the least work in the longest space of time. That is the difference. Free labor, love, affection—they have invented everything of use in this world. I am a Republican.

I tell you, my friends, this world is getting better every day, and the Democratic party is getting smaller every day. See the advancement we have made in a few years, see what we have done. We have covered this nation with wealth, and glory, and with liberty. This is the first free government in the world. The Republican party is the first party that was not founded on some compromise with the devil. It is the first party of pure, square, honest principle; the first one. And we have got the first free country that ever existed.

And right here I want to thank every soldier that fought to make it free, every one living and dead. I want to thank you again, and again, and again. You made the first free government in the world, and we must not forget the dead heroes. If they were here they would vote the Republican ticket, every one of them. I tell you we must not forget them.

The past, as it were, rises before me like a dream. Again
we are in the great struggle for national life. We hear the
sound of preparation—the music of the boisterous drums—
the silver voices of heroic bugles. We see thousands of
assemblages, and hear the appeals of orators; we see the
pale cheeks of women, and the flushed faces of men ; and
in those assemblages we see all the dead whose dust we
have covered with flowers. We lose sight of them no
more. We are with them when they enlist in the great
army of freedom. We see them part with those they love.
Some are walking for the last time in quiet woody places
with the maidens they adore. We hear the whisperings
and the sweet vows of eternal love as they lingeringly
part forever. Others are bending over cradles kissing
babes that are asleep. Some are receiving the blessings of
old men. Some are parting with mothers who hold them
and press them to their hearts again and again, and say
nothing ; and some are talking with wives, and endeavoring
with brave words spoken in the old tones to drive away the
awful fear. We see them part. We see the wife standing
in the door with the babe in her arms—standing in the sunlight sobbing—at the turn of the road a hand waves—she
answers by holding high in her loving hands the child. He
is gone, and forever.

We see them all as they march proudly away under the
flaunting flags, keeping time to the wild grand music of
war—marching down the streets of the great cities—through
the towns and across the prairies—down to the fields of
glory, to do and to die for the eternal right.

We go with them one and all. We are by their side on
all the gory fields, in all the hospitals of pain—on all the

weary marches. We stand guard with them in the wild
storm and under the quiet stars. We are with them in
ravines running with blood—in the furrows of old fields.
We are with them between contending hosts, unable to
move, wild with thirst, the life ebbing slowly away among
the withered leaves. We see them pierced by balls and
torn with shells in the trenches of forts, and in the whirlwind of the charge, where men become iron with nerves
of steel.

We are with them in the prisons of hatred and famine,
but human speech can never tell what they endured.

We are at home when the news comes that they are dead.
We see the maiden in the shadow of her sorrow. We see
the silvered head of the old man bowed with the last grief.

The past rises before us, and we see four millions of
human beings governed by the lash—we see them bound
hand and foot—we hear the strokes of cruel whips—we see
the hounds tracking women through tangled swamps. We
see babes sold from the breasts of mothers. Cruelty unspeakable! Outrage infinite!

Four million bodies in chains—four million souls in fetters.
All the sacred relations of wife, mother, father and child,
trampled beneath the brutal feet of might. And all this
was done under our own beautiful banner of the free.

The past rises before us. We hear the roar and shriek of
the bursting shell. The broken fetters fall. There heroes
died. We look. Instead of slaves we see men and
women and children. The wand of progress touches the
auction-block, the slave-pen, and the whipping-post, and we
see homes and firesides, and school-houses and books, and
where all was want and crime, and cruelty and fear, we see
the faces of the free.

These heroes are dead. They died for liberty—they
died for us. They are at rest. They sleep in the land they

made free, under the flag they rendered stainless, under the solemn pines, the sad hemlocks, the tearful willows, the embracing vines. They sleep beneath the shadows of the clouds, careless alike of sunshine or storm, each in the windowless palace of rest. Earth may run red with other wars—they are at peace. In the midst of battle, in the roar of conflict, they found the serenity of death. I have one sentiment for the soldiers living and dead—cheers for the living and tears for the dead.

MORE SOLID SHOT.

Now, my friends, I have given you a few reasons why I am a Republican. I have given you a few reasons why I am not a Democrat. Let me say another thing. The Democratic party opposed every movement of the army of the Republic, every one. Don't be fooled. Imagine the meanest resolution that you can think of—that is the resolution the Democratic party passed. Imagine the meanest thing you can think of—that is what they did; and I want you to recollect that the Democratic party did these devilish things when the fate of this nation was trembling in the balance of war. I want you to recollect another thing; when they tell you about hard times, that the Democratic party made the hard times; that every dollar we owe to-day was made by the Southern and Northern Democracy.

When we commenced to put down the rebellion we had to borrow money, and the Democratic party went into the markets of the world and impaired the credit of the United States. They slandered, they lied, they maligned the credit of the United States, and to such an extent did they do this, that at one time during the war paper was only worth about 34 cents on the dollar. Gold went up to $2.90. What did that mean? It meant that greenbacks were worth

34 cents on the dollar. What became of the other 66 cents? They were lied out of the greenbacks, they were calumniated out of the greenbacks, by the Democratic party of the North. Two-thirds of the debt, two-thirds of the burden now upon the shoulders of American industry, were placed there by the slanders of the Democratic party of the North, and the other third by the Democratic party of the South. And when you pay your taxes keep an account and charge two-thirds to the Northern Democracy and one-third to the Southern Democracy, and whenever you have to earn the money to pay the taxes, when you have to blister your hands to earn that money, pull off the blisters, and under each one, as the foundation, you will find a Democratic lie.

Recollect that the Democratic party did all the things of which I have told you, when the fate of our nation was submitted to the arbitrament of the sword. Recollect they did these things when your husbands, your fathers, your brothers, your chivalric sons were fighting, bleeding, suffering upon the fields of the South, where shot and shell were crashing through their sacred flesh, where they were lying upon the field of battle, the blood slowly oozing from the pallid, mangled lips of death; when they were in the hospitals of pain, dreaming broken dreams of home, and seeing fever pictures of the ones they loved; when they were in the prison pens of the South, with no covering but the clouds, no bed except the frozen earth, no food except such as worms had refused to eat, and no friends except insanity and death. Recollect it. I have often said that I wished there were words of pure hatred out of which I might construct sentences like serpents, sentences like snakes, sentences that would writhe and hiss—I could then give my opinion of the Northern allies of the Southern rebels.

There are three questions now submitted to the American people. The first is, Shall the people that saved this country rule it? Shall the men who saved the old flag hold it? Shall the men who saved the ship of State sail it? or shall the rebels walk her quarter-deck, give the orders and sink it. That is the question. Shall a solid South, a united South, united by assassination and murder, a South solidified by the shot-gun; shall a united South, with the aid of a divided North, shall they control this great and splendid country? Well, then the North must wake up. We are right back where we were in 1861. This is simply a prolongation of the war. This is the war of the idea, the other was the war of the musket. The other was the war of cannon, this is the war of thought; and we have got to beat them in this war of thought, recollect that. The question is, Shall the men who endeavored to destroy this country rule it? Shall the men that said, This is not a nation, have charge of the nation?

The next question is, Shall we pay our debts? We had to borrow some money to pay for shot and shell to shoot Democrats with. We found that we could get along with a few less Democrats, but not with any less country, and so we borrowed the money, and the question now is, will we pay it? And which party is the most apt to pay it, the Republican party, that made the debt—the party that swore it was constitutional, or the party that said it was unconstitutional? Whenever a Democrat sees a greenback, the greenback says to the Democrat, " I am one of the fellows that whipped you." Whenever a Republican sees a greenback, the greenback says to him, " You and I put down the rebellion and saved the country." Now, my friends, you have heard a great deal about finances. Nearly everybody that talks about it gets as dry——as if they had been in the final home of the Democratic party for forty years.

I will give you my ideas about finances. In the first place the government don't support the people ; the people support the government. The government passes around the hat, the government passes around the alms dish. True enough, it has a musket behind it, but it is a perpetual, chronic pauper. It passes, I told you, the alms-dish, and we all throw in our share—except Tilden. This government is a perpetual consumer. You understand me, the government don't plow ground, the government don't raise corn and wheat ; the government is simply a perpetual consumer ; we support the government. Now, the idea that the government can make money for you and I to live on—why. it is the same as though my hired man should issue certificates of my indebtedness to him for me to live on.

Some people tell me that the government can impress its sovereignty on a piece of paper, and that is money. Well, if it is, what's the use of wasting it making one dollar bills? It takes no more ink and no more paper—why not make $1000 bills? Why not make $100,000,000 bills and all be billionaires ?

If the government can make money, what on earth does it collect taxes from you and me for? Why don't it make what money it wants, take the taxes out, and give the balance to us? Mr. Greenbacker, suppose the government issued $1,000,000,000 to-morrow, how would you get any of it? (A voice—Steal it.) I was not speaking to the Democrats.—You would not get any of it unless you had something to exchange for it. The government would not go around and give you your average. You have to have some corn, or wheat, or pork to give for it.

How do you get your money? By work. Where from? You have to dig it out of the ground. That is whe? it comes from. In old times there were some men who th ught they could get some way to turn the baser metals into g ld. and old gray-haired men, trembling, tottering on the verge of the grave, were hunting for something to turn ordinary metals into gold; they were searching for the fountain of eternal youth, but they did not find it. No human ear has ever heard the silver gurgle of the spring of immortal youth.

There used to be mechanics that tried to make perpetual motion by combinations of wheels, shifting weights, and rolling balls; but somehow the machine would never quite run. A perpetual fountain of greenbacks, of wealth without labor, is just as foolish as a fountain of eternal youth. The idea that you can produce money without labor is just as foolish as the idea of perpetual motion. They are old follies under new names.

Let me tell you another thing. The Democrats seem to think that you can fail to keep a promise so long that it is as good as though you had kept it. They say you can stamp the sovereignty of the government upon paper. The other day I saw a piece of silver bearing the sovereign stamp of Julius Cæsar. Julius Cæsar has been dust about two thousand years, but that piece of silver was worth just as much as though Julius Cæsar was at the head of the Roman legions. Was it his sovereignty that made it valuable? Suppose he had put it upon a piece of paper—it would have been of no more value than a Democratic promise.

Another thing, my friends, this debt will be paid; you need not worry about that. The Democrats ought to pay

it. They lost the suit and they ought to pay the costs.
But we are willing to pay our share. It will be paid. The
holders of the debt have got a mortgage on a continent.
They have a mortgage on the honor of the Republican
party, and it is on record. Every blade of grass that
grows upon this continent is a guarantee that the debt will
be paid; every field of bannered corn in the great, glorious
West is a guarantee that the debt will be paid; all the coal
put away in the ground millions of years ago by that old
miser, the sun, is a guarantee that every dollar of that debt
will be paid; all the cattle on the prairies, pastures and
plains, every one of them is a guarantee that this debt will
be paid; every pine standing in the somber forests of the
North, waiting for the woodman's ax, is a guarantee that
this debt will be paid; all the gold and silver hid in the
Sierra Nevadas, waiting for the miner's pick, is a guarantee that the debt will be paid; every locomotive, with its
muscles of iron and breath of flame, and all the boys and
girls bending over their books at school, every dimpled
child in the cradle, every good man and every good woman,
and every man that votes the Republican ticket is a guarantee that the debt will be paid.

MORE ELOQUENCE.

What is the next question? The next question is, will
we protect the Union men in the South? I tell you the
white Union men have suffered enough. It is a crime in
the Southern States to be a Republican. It is a crime in
every Southern State to love this country, to believe in the
sacred rights of men.

I tell you the colored people have suffered enough. They
have been owned by Democrats for two hundred years.
Worse than that: they have been forced to keep the company of their owners. It is a terrible thing to live with a

man that steals from you. They have suffered enough. For two hundred years they were branded like cattle. Yes, for two hundred years every human tie was torn asunder by the cruel hand of avarice and greed. For two hundred years children were sold from their mothers, husbands from their wives, brothers from brothers, and sisters from sisters. There was not during the whole rebellion a single negro that was not our friend. We are willing to be reconciled to our Southern brethren when they will treat our friends as men. When they will be just to the friends of this country; when they are in favor of allowing every American citizen to have his rights—then we are their friends. We are willing to trust them with the Nation when they are the friends of the Nation. We are willing to trust them with liberty when they believe in liberty. We are willing to trust them with the black man when they cease riding in the darkness of night—those masked wretches—to the hut of the freedman, and notwithstanding the prayers and supplications of his family, shoot him down; when they cease to consider the massacre of Hamburg as a Democratic triumph, then, I say, we will be their friends, and not before.

Now, my friends, thousands of the Southern people, and thousands of the Northern Democrats, are afraid that the negroes are going to pass them in the race for life. And, Mr. Democrat, he will do it unless you attend to your business. The simple fact that you are white cannot save you always. You have got to be industrious, honest, to cultivate a justice. If you don't the colored race will pass you, as sure as you live. I am for giving every man a chance. Anybody that can pass me is welcome.

I believe, my friends, that the intellectual domain of the future, like the land used to be in the State of Illinois, is open to pre-emption. The fellow that gets a fact first, that is his ; that gets an idea first, that is his. Every round in the ladder of fame, from the one that touches the ground to the last one that leans against the shining summit of ambition, belongs to the foot that gets upon it first.

Mr. Democrat,—I point down because they are nearly all on the first round of the ladder,—if you can't climb, stand one side and let the deserving negro pass.

INGERSOLL'S BIG HORSE-RACE.

I must tell you one thing. I have told it so much, and you have all heard it, I have no doubt, fifty times from others, but I am going to tell it again because I like it.

Suppose there was a great horse-race here to-day, free to every horse in the world, and to all the mules, and all the scrubs, and all the donkeys. At the tap of the drum they come to the line, and the judges say "it is a go." Let me ask you, what does the blooded horse, rushing ahead, with nostrils distended, drinking in the breath of his own swiftness, with his mane flying like a banner of victory, with his veins standing out all over him, as if a net of life had been cast around him—with his thin neck, his high withers, his tremulous flanks—what does he care how many mules and donkeys run on that track? But the Democratic scrub, with his chuckle head and lop-ears, with his tail full of cuckle-burs, jumping high and short, and digging in the ground when he feels the breath of the coming mule on his cuckle-bur tail, he is the chap that jumps the track and says, "I am down on mule equality."

My friends, the Republican party is the blooded horse in this race.

I stood, a little while ago, in the city of Paris, where stood the Bastile, where now stands the column of July, surmounted by the figure of liberty. In its right hand is a broken chain, in its left hand a banner; upon its shining forehead a glittering star—and as I looked upon it I said, such is the Republican party of my country. The other day going along the road I came to the place where the road had been changed, but the guide-board was as they had put it twenty years before. It pointed diligently in the direction of a desolate field. Now, that guide-post had been there for twenty years. Thousands of people passed, but nobody heeded the hand on the guide-post, and it stuck there through storm and shine, and it pointed as hard as ever as if the road was through the desolate field; and I said to myself, such is the Democratic party of the United States.

The other day I came to a river where there had been a mill; a part of it was there yet. An old sign said, "Cash for wheat." The old water-wheel was broken, and it had been warped by the sun, cracked and split by many winds and storms. There hadn't been a grain of wheat ground there for twenty years. There was nothing in good order but the dam; it was as good a dam as ever I saw, and I said to myself, "such is the Democratic party." I was going along the road the other day, when I came to where there had once been a hotel. But the hotel and barn had burned down; nothing remained but the two chimneys, monuments of the disaster. In the road there was an old sign, upon which were these words: "Entertainment for man and beast." The word "man" was nearly burned out. There hadn't been a hotel there for thirty years. That sign had swung and creaked in the wind; the snow had fallen upon it in the winter, the birds had sung upon it in the summer. Nobody ever stopped at that hotel; but the sign stuck to it and kept swearing to it, "Entertainment for man and beast," and I said to myself, "Such is the Democratic party of the United States."

Now, my friends, I want you to vote the Republican

ticket. I want you to swear you will not vote for a man who opposed putting down the rebellion. I want you to swear that you will not vote for a man opposed to the utter abolition of slavery. I want you to swear that you will not vote for a man who called the soldiers in the field Lin-coln hirelings. I want you to swear that you will not vote for a man who denounced Lincoln as a tyrant. I want you to swear that you will not vote for any enemy of human progress. Go and talk to every Democrat that you can see; get him by the coat-collar, talk to him, and hold him like Coleridge's Ancient mariner, with your glittering eye; hold him, tell him all the mean things his party ever did; tell him kindly; tell him in a Christian spirit, as I do, but tell him. Recollect there never was a more important election than the one you are going to hold in Indiana. I want you every one to swear that you will vote for glorious Ben Harrison. I tell you we must stand by the country. It is a glorious country. It permits you and me to be free. It is the only country in the world where labor is respected. Let us support it. It is the only country in the world where the useful man is the only aristocrat. The man that works for a dollar a day, goes home at night to his little ones, taking his little boy on his knee, and he thinks that boy can achieve anything that the sons of the wealthy man can achieve. The free schools are open to him; he may be the richest, the greatest, and the grandest, and that thought sweetens every drop of sweat that rolls down the honest face of toil. Vote to save that country.

INGERSOLL'S BEAUTIFUL DREAM.

My friends, this country is getting better every day. Samuel J. Tilden says we are a nation of thieves and rascals If that is so he ought to be the President. But I denounce him as a calumniator of my country; a maligner of this nation. It is not so. This country is covered with asylums for the aged, the helpless, the insane, the orphan, wounded soldiers. Thieves and rascals don't build such things. In the cities of the Atlantic coast this summer, they built floating hospitals, great ships, and took the little children from the sub-cellars and narrow, dirty streets of New York city, where the Democratic party is the strongest,—took these poor waifs and put them in these great hospitals out at sea, and let the breezes of ocean kiss the roses of health back to their pallid cheeks. Rascals and thieves do not do so. When Chicago burned, railroads were blocked with the charity of the American people. Thieves and rascals did not do so.

I am a Republican. The world is getting better. Husbands are treating their wives better than they used to; wives are treating their husbands better. Children are better treated than they used to be; the old whips and gods are out of the schools, and they are governing children by love and by sense. The world is getting better; it is getting better in Maine. It has got better in Maine, in Vermont. It is getting better in every State of the North.

I have a dream that this world is growing better and better every day and every year; that there is more charity, more justice, more love every day. I have a dream that prisons will not always curse the earth; that the shadow of the gallows will not always fall on the land; that the withered hand of want will not always be stretched out for charity; that finally wisdom will sit in the legislature, justice in the courts, charity will occupy all the pulpits, and that finally the world will be controlled by liberty and love, by justice and charity. That is my dream, and if it does not come true, it shall not be my fault. Good-bye. (Immense and prolonged cheering.)

III.—CCL. INGERSOLL'S GREAT SPEECH ON THE DECLARATION OF INDEPENDENCE.

THE GRANDEST OF DOCUMENTS.

[*From the Indianapolis Journal.*]

LADIES AND GENTLEMEN: The Declaration of Inde-pendence is the grandest, the bravest, and the profoundest political document that was ever signed by the representatives of the people. It is the embodiment of physical and moral courage and of political wisdom.

I say physical courage, because it was a declaration of war against the most powerful nation then on the globe; a declaration of war by thirteen weak, unorganized colonies; a declaration of war by a few people, without military stores, without wealth, without strength, against the most powerful kingdom on the earth; a declaration of war made when the British navy, at that day the mistress of every sea, was hovering along the coast of America, looking after defenseless towns and villages to ravage and destroy. It was made when thousands of English soldiers were upon our soil, and when the principal cities of America were in the substantial possession of the enemy. And so, I say, all things considered, it was the bravest political document ever signed by man. And if it was physically brave, the moral courage of the document is almost infinitely beyond the physical. They had the courage not only, but they

47

had the almost infinite wisdom, to declare that all men are created equal.

With one blow, with one stroke of the pen, they struck down all the cruel, heartless barriers that aristocracy, that priestcraft, that kingcraft had raised between man and man. They struck down with one immortal blow that infamous spirit of caste that makes a god almost a beast, and a beast almost a god. With one word, with one blow, they wiped away and utterly destroyed all that had been done by centuries of war—centuries of hypocrisy—centuries of injustice.

What more did they do? Then they declared that each man has a right to live. And what does that mean? It means that he has the right to make his living. It means that he has the right to breathe the air, to work the land, that he stands the equal of every other human being beneath the shining stars; entitled to the product of his labor —the labor of his hand and of his brain.

What more? That every man has the right to pursue his own happiness in his own way. Grander words than these have never been spoken by man.

And what more did these men say? They laid down the doctrine that governments were instituted among men for the purpose of preserving the rights of the people. The old idea was that people existed solely for the benefit of the State—that is to say, for kings and nobles.

The old idea was that the people were the wards of king and priest—that their bodies belonged to one and their souls to the other.

A REVELATION AND REVOLUTION.

And what more? That the people are the source of political power. That was not only a revelation, but it was a revolution. It changed the ideas of people with regard to the source of political power. For the first time it made human beings men. What was the old idea? The old idea was that no political power came from, nor in any manner belonged to, the people. The old idea was that the political power came from the clouds; that the political power came in some miraculous way from heaven; that it came down to kings, and queens, and robbers. That was the old idea. The nobles lived upon the labor of the people; the people had no rights; the nobles stole what they had and divided with the kings, and the kings pretended to divide what they stole with God Almighty. The source, then, of political power was from above. The people were responsible to the nobles, the nobles to the king, and the people had no political rights whatever, no more than the wild beasts of the forest. The kings were responsible to God, not to the people. The kings were responsible to the clouds, not to the toiling millions they robbed and plundered.

And our forefathers, in this declaration of independence, reversed this thing, and said: No, the people, they are the source of political power, and their rulers, these presidents, these kings, are but the agents and servants of the great, sublime people. For the first time, really, in the history of the world, the king was made to get off the throne and the people were royally seated thereon. The people became the sovereigns, and the old sovereigns became the servants and the agents of the people. It is hard for you and me now to imagine even the immense results of that change. It is hard for you and me, at this day, to understand how thoroughly it had been ingrained in the brain of almost every man, that the king had some wonderful right over him; that in some strange way the king owned him; that in some miraculous manner he belonged, body and soul, to somebody who rode on a horse, to somebody with epaulettes on his shoulders, and a tinsel crown upon his brainless head.

Our forefathers had been educated in that idea, and when they first landed on American shores they believed it. They thought they belonged to somebody, and that they must be loyal to some thief, who could trace his pedigree back to antiquity's most successful robber.

It took a long time for them to get that idea out of their heads and hearts. They were three thousand miles away from the despotisms of the old world, and every wave of the sea was an assistant to them. The distance helped to disenchant their minds of that infamous belief, and every mile between them and the pomp and glory of monarchy helped to put republican ideas and thoughts into their minds. Besides that, when they came to this country, when the savage was in the forest and three thousand miles of waves on the other side, menaced by barbarians on the one side, and famine on the other, they learned that a man who had courage, a man who had thought, was as good as any other man in the world, and they built up, as it were, in spite of themselves, little republics. And the man that had the most nerve and heart was the best man, whether he had any noble blood in his veins or not.

THE EDUCATION OF NATURE.

It has been a favorite idea with me that our forefathers were educated by nature; that they grew grand as the continent upon which they landed; that the great rivers— the wide plains—the splendid lakes—the lonely forests— the sublime mountains—that all these things stole into and became a part of their being, and they grew great as the country in which they lived. They began to hate the narrow, contracted views of Europe. They were educated by their surroundings, and every little colony had to be,

to a certain extent, a republic. The kings of the old
world endeavored to parcel out this land to their favorites.
But there were too many Indians. There was too much
courage required for them to take and keep it, and so men
had to come here who were dissatisfied with the old country
—who were dissatisfied with England, dissatisfied with
France, with Germany, with Ireland and Holland. The
kings' favorites stayed at home. Men came here for liberty,
and on account of certain principles they entertained and
held dearer than life. And they were willing to work,
willing to fell the forests, to fight the savages, willing to go
through all the hardships, perils and dangers of a new
country, of a new land ; and the consequence was that our
country was settled by brave and adventurous spirits, by
men who had opinions of their own, and were willing to
live in the wild forests for the sake of expressing those
opinions, even if they expressed them only to trees, rocks,
and savage men. The best blood of the old world came to
the new.

THE RISE OF THE REPUBLIC—LIBERTY AND TOLERATION.

When they first came over they did not have a great deal
of political philosophy, nor the best ideas of liberty. We
might as well tell the truth. When the puritans first came
they were narrow. They did not understand what liberty
meant— what religious liberty, what political liberty, was;
but they found out in a few years. There was one feeling
among them that rises to their eternal honor like a white
shaft to the clouds—they were in favor of universal education. Wherever they went they built school houses, intro-
duced books, and ideas of literature. They believed that
every man should know how to read and how to write, and
should find out all that his capacity allowed him to comprehend. That is the glory of the Puritan fathers.

Tney forgot in a little while what they had suffered, and they forgot to apply the principle of universal liberty—of toleration. Some of the colonies did not forget it, and I want to give credit where credit should be given. The Catholics of Maryland were the first people on the new continent to declare universal religious toleration. Let this be remembered to their eternal honor. Let it be remembered to the disgrace of the Protestant government of England, that it caused this grand law to be repealed. And to the honor and credit of the Catholics of Maryland let it be remembered, that the moment they got back into power they re-enacted the old law. The Baptists of Rhode Island, also, led by Roger Williams, were in favor of universal religious liberty.

No American should fail to honor Roger Williams. He was the first grand advocate of the liberty of the soul. He was in favor of the eternal divorce of Church and State. So far as I know, he was the only man at that time in this country who was in favor of real religious liberty. While the Catholics of Maryland declared in favor of religious *toleration*, they had no idea of religious liberty. They would not allow any one to call in question the doctrine of the trinity, or the inspiration of the scriptures. They stood ready with branding-iron and gallows to burn and choke out of man the idea that he had a right to think and to express his thoughts.

So many religions met in our country—so many theories and dogmas came in contact—so many follies, mistakes and stupidities became acquainted with each other, that religion began to fall somewhat into dispute. Besides this, the question of a new nation began to take precedence of all others.

The people were too much interested in this world to quarrel about the next. The preacher was lost in the patriot. The bible was read to find passages against kings.

Everybody was discussing the rights of man. Farmers and mechanics suddenly became statesmen, and in every shop and cabin nearly every question was asked and answered.

During these years of political excitement, the interest in religion abated to that degree that a common purpose animated men of all sects and creeds.

At last our fathers became tired of being colonists—tired of writing and reading and signing petitions, and presenting them, on their bended knees, to an idiot king. They began to have an aspiration to form a new nation, to be citizens of a new republic instead of subjects to an old monarchy. They had the idea—the Puritans, the Catholics, the Episcopalians, the Baptists, the Quakers, and a few Free-Thinkers, all had the idea—that they would like to form a new nation.

Now, do not understand that all of our fathers were in favor of independence. Do not understand that they were all like Jefferson; that they were all like Adams or Lee; that they were all like Thomas Paine or John Hancock. There were thousands and thousands of them who were opposed to American independence. There were thousands and thousands who said: "When you say men are created equal, it is a lie; when you say the political power resides in the great body of the people, it is false." Thousands and thousands of them said: "We prefer Great Britain." But the men who were in favor of independence, the men who knew that a new nation must be born, went on full of hope and courage, and nothing could daunt or stop or stay the heroic, fearless few.

They met in Philadelphia, and the resolution was moved by Lee, of Virginia, that the colonies ought to be independent States, and ought to dissolve their political connection with Great Britain.

They made up their minds that a new nation must be formed. All nations had been, so to speak, the wards of some church. The religious idea as to the source of power had been at the foundation of all governments, and had been the bane and curse of man.

Happily for us, there was no church strong enough to dictate to the rest. Fortunately for us, the colonists not only, but the colonies differed widely in their religious views. There were the Puritans who hated the Episcopalians, and Episcopalians who hated the Catholics, and the Catholics who hated both, while the Quakers held them all in contempt. There they were, of every sort, and color, and kind, and how was it that they came together? They had a common aspiration. They wanted to form a new nation. More than that, most of them cordially hated Great Britain; and they pledged each other to forget these religious preiudices, for a time at least, and agreed that there should be only one religion until they got through, and that was the religion of patriotism. They solemnly agreed that the new nation should not belong to any particular church, but that it should secure the rights of all.

Our fathers founded the first secular government that was ever founded in this world. Recollect that. The first secular government; the first government that said every church has exactly the same rights, and no more; every religion has the same rights and no more. In other words our fathers were the first men who had the sense, had the genius, to know that no church should be allowed to have a sword; that it should be allowed only to exert its moral influence.

You might as well have a government united by force with Art, or with Poetry, or with Oratory, as with Religion. Religion should have the influence upon mankind that its goodness, that its morality, its justice, its charity, its reason and its argument give it, and no more. Religion should have the effect upon mankind that it necessarily has, and no more.

So our fathers said: "We shall form a secular government, and under the flag with which we are going to enrich the air, we will allow every man to worship God as he thinks best." They said: "Religion is an individual thing between each man and his Creator, and he can worship as he pleases and as he desires." And why did they do this? The history of the world warned them that the liberty of man was not safe in the clutch and grasp of any church. They had read of and seen the thumb-screws, the racks and the dungeons of the inquisition. They knew all about the hypocrisy of the olden time. They knew that the church had stood side by side with the throne: that the high priests were hypocrites, and that the kings were robbers. They also knew that if they gave to any church power, it would corrupt the best church in the world. And so the said that power must not reside in a church, nor in a sect, but power must be wherever humanity is—in the great body of the people. And the officers and servants of the people must be responsible to them. And so I say again, as I said in the commencement, this is the wisest, the profoundest, the bravest political document that ever was written and signed by man.

They turned, as I tell you, everything squarely about. They derived all their authority from the people. They did away forever with the theological idea of government. And what more did they say? They said that whenever the rulers abused this authority, this power, incapable of destruction, returned to the people. How did they come to say this? I will tell you; they were pushed into it

How? They felt that they were oppressed; and whenever a man feels that he is the subject of injustice, his perception of right and wrong is wonderfully quickened.

Nobody was ever in prison wrongfully who did not believe in the writ of *habeas corpus.* Nobody ever suffered wrongfully without instantly having ideas of justice.

And they began to inquire what rights the king of Great Britain had. They began to search for the charter of his authority. They began to investigate and dig down to the bed-rock upon which society must be founded, and when they got there, forced there, too, by their oppressors, forced against their own prejudices and education, they found at the bottom of things, not lords, not nobles, not pulpits, not thrones, but humanity, and the rights of men.

And so they said, we are men; we are MEN.

A NATION.

They found out they were men. And the next thing they said was: "We will be free men; we are weary of being colonists; we are tired of being subjects; we are men; and these colonies ought to be states; and these states ought to be a nation; and that nation ought to drive the last British soldier into the sea." And so they signed that brave declaration of independence.

I thank every one of them from the bottom of my heart for signing that sublime declaration. I thank them for their courage—for their patriotism—for their wisdom—for the splendid confidence in themselves and in the human race. I thank them for what they were, and for what we are—for what they did, and for what we have received—for what they suffered, and for what we enjoy.

What would we have been if we had remained colonists and subjects? What would we have been to-day? Nobodies—ready to get down on our knees and crawl in the very dust at the sight of somebody that was supposed to have in him some drop of blood that flowed in the veins of that mailed marauder —William the Conqueror.

They signed that declaration of independence, although they knew that it would produce a long, terrible, and bloody war. They looked forward and saw poverty, depri-vation, gloom, and death. But they also saw, on the wrecked clouds of war, the beautiful bow of freedom.

These grand men were enthusiasts; and the world has only been raised by enthusiasts. In every country there have been a few who have given a national aspiration to the people. The enthusiasts of 1776 were the builders and framers of this great and splendid government; and they were the men who saw, although others did not, the golden fringe of the mantle of glory, that will finally cover this world. They knew, they felt, they believed they would give a new constellation to the political heavens—that they would make the Americans a grand people—grand as the continent upon which they lived.

The war commenced. There was little money and less credit. The new nation had but few friends. To a great extent, each soldier of freedom had to clothe and feed him-self. He was poor and pure—brave and good, and so he went to the fields of death to fight for the rights of man.

What did the soldier leave when he went? He left his wife and children.

Did he leave them in a beautiful home, surrounded by civilization, in the repose of law, in the security of a great and powerful republic?

No. He left his wife and children on the edge, on the fringe of the boundless forest, in which crouched and crept the red savage, who was at that time the ally of the still more savage Briton. He left his wife to defend herself, and he left the prattling babes to be defended by their mother and by nature. The mother made the living; she

planted the corn and the potatoes, and hoed them in the
sun, raised the children, and in the dark night told them
about their brave father, and the "sacred cause," she told
them that in a little while the war would be over, and father
would come back covered with honor and glory.

Think of the women, of the sweet children who listened
for the footsteps of the dead—who waited through the sad
and desolated years for the dear ones who never came.

LIBERTY OR DEATH.

The soldiers of 1776 did not march away with music and
banners. They went in silence, looked at and gazed after
by eyes filled with tears. They went to meet, not an equal,
but a superior—to fight five times their number—to make a
desperate stand—to stop the advance of the enemy, and
then, when their ammunition gave out, seek the protection
of rocks, of rivers, and of hills.

Let me say here: The greatest test of courage on the
earth is to bear defeat without losing heart. That army is
the bravest that can be whipped the greatest number of
times and fight again.

Over the entire territory, so to speak, then settled by our
forefathers, they were driven again and again. Now and
then they would meet the English with something like equal
numbers, and then the eagle of victory would proudly perch
upon the stripes and stars. And so they went on as best
they could, hoping and fighting until they came to the dark
and somber gloom of Valley Forge.

There were very few hearts then beneath that flag that
did not begin to think that the struggle was useless; that
all the blood and treasure had been spent and shed in vain.
But there were some men gifted with that wonderful proph-
ecy that fulfills itself, and with that wonderful magnetic
power that makes heroes of everybody they come in contact
with. And so our fathers went through the gloom of that ter-

rible time, and still fought on. Brave men wrote g˙and
words, cheering the despondent; brave men did brave
deeds; the rich man gave his wealth; the poor man gave
his life, until at last, by the victory of Yorktown, the old
banner won its place in the air, and became glorious forever.

Seven long years of war—fighting for what? For the
principle that all men are created equal—a truth that nobody ever disputed except a scoundrel; nobody in the
entire history of this world. No man ever denied *that*
truth who was not a rascal, and at heart a thief; never,
never, and never will. What else were they fighting for?
Simply that in America every man should have a right to
life, liberty and the pursuit of happiness. Nobody ever
denied that except a villian; never, never. It has been
denied by kings—they were thieves. It has been denied
by statesmen—they were liars. It has been denied by
priests, by clergymen, by cardinals, by bishops and by
popes—they were hypocrites.

What else were they fighting for? For the idea that all
political power is vested in the great body of the people.
They make all the money; do all the work. They plow
the land; cut down the forests; they produce everything
that is produced. Then who shall say what shall be done
with what is produced except the producer? Is it the non-
producing thief, sitting on a throne, surrounded by vermin?

The history of civilization is the history of the slow and
painful enfranchisement of the human race. In the elden
times the family was a monarchy, the father being the monarch. The mother and children were the veriest slaves.
The will of the father was the supreme law. He had the
power of life and death. It took thousands of years to civilize this father, thousands of years to make the condition of
wife and mother and children even tolerable. A few families constituted a tribe; the tribe had a chief; the chief

protect the rights of others. It is a sublime thing to be free and just.

Only a few days ago I stood in Independence Hall—in that little room where was signed the immortal paper. A little room, like any other; and it did not seem possible that from that room went forth ideas, like cherubim and seraphim, spreading their wings over a continent, and touching, as with holy fire, the hearts of men.

In a few moments I was in the park, where are gathered the accomplishments of a century. Our fathers never dreamed of the things I saw. There were hundreds of locomotives, with their nerves of steel and breath of flame—every kind of machine, with whirling wheels and the myriad thoughts of men that have been wrought in iron, brass and steel. And going out from one little building were wires in the air, stretching to every civilized nation, and they could send a shining messenger in a moment to any part of the world, and it would go sweeping under the waves of the sea with thoughts and words within its glowing heart I saw all that had been achieved by this nation, and I wished that the signers of the Declaration—the soldiers of the Revolution—could see what a century of freedom has produced. I wished they could see the fields we cultivate—the rivers we navigate—the railroads running over the Alleghanies, far into what was then the unknown forest—on over the broad prairies—on over the vast plains—away over the mountains of the West, to the Golden Gate of the Pacific.

All this is the result of a hundred years of freedom. Are you not more than glad that in 1776 was announced the sublime principle that political power resides with the people? that our fathers then made up their minds nevermore to be colonists and subjects, but that they would be free and independent citizens of America. I will not name any of the grand men who fought for liberty. All should be named, or none. I feel that the unknown soldier who was shot down without even his name being remembered—who was included only in a report of "a hundred killed," or "a hundred missing," nobody knowing even the number that attached to his august corpse—is entitled to as deep and heartfelt thanks as the titled leader who fell at the head of the host.

THE GRAND FUTURE OF AMERICA.

Standing here amid the sacred memories of the first, on the golden threshold of the second, I ask, Will the second century be as grand as the first? I believe it will, because we are growing more and more humane; I believe there is more human kindness, and a greater desire to help one another, than in all the world besides.

We must progress. We are just at the commencement of invention. The steam engine—the telegraph—these are but the toys with which science has been amused. There will be grander things; there will be wider and higher culture—a grander standard of character, of literature and art.

We have now half as many millions of people as we have years. We are getting more real solid sense. We are writing and reading more books; we are struggling more and more to get at the philosophy of life, of things—trying more and more to answer the questions of the eternal Sphinx. We are looking in every direction—investigating; in short, we are thinking and working.

The world has changed. I have had the supreme pleasure of seeing a man—once a slave—sitting in the seat of his former master in the Congress of the United States. I have had that pleasure, and when I saw it my eyes were filled with tears, I felt that we had carried out the Declaration of Independence, that we have given reality to it, and breathed the breath of life into its every word. I felt that our flag would float over and protect the colored man and his little children—standing straight in the sun, just the same as though he were white and worth a million.

All who stand beneath our banner are free. Ours is the only flag that has in reality written upon it: Liberty, Fraternity, Equality—the three grandest words in all the languages of men. Liberty: Give to every man the fruit of his own labor—the labor of his hand and of his brain. Fraternity: Every man in the right is my brother. Equality: The rights of all are equal. No race, no color, no previous condition, can change the rights of men. The Declaration of Independence has at last been carried out in letter and in spirit. The second century will be grander than the first. To-day the black man looks upon his child and says: The avenues of distinction are open to you—upon your brow may fall the civic wreath. We are celebrating the courage and wisdom of our fathers, and the glad shout of a free people, the anthem of a grand nation, commencing at the Atlantic, is following the sun to the Pacific, across a continent of happy homes. We are a great people. Three millions have increased to fifty—thirteen states to thirty-eight. We have better homes, and more of the conveniences of life than any other people upon the face of the globe. The farmers of our country live better than did the kings and princes two hundred years ago—and they have twice as much sense and heart. Liberty and labor have given us all. Remember that all men have equal rights. Remember that the man who acts best his part—who loves his friends the best—is most willing to help others—truest to the obligation—who has the best heart—the most feeling—the deepest sympathies—and who freely gives to others the rights that he claims for himself, is the best man. We have disfranchised the aristocrats of the air and have given one country to mankind.

Col. Ingersoll's Funeral Oration at His Brother's Grave.

The funeral of Hon. Ebon C. Ingersoll, brother of Col. Robert G. Ingersoll, took place at his residence in Washington, D. C., June 2, 1879. The ceremonies were extremely simple, consisting merely of viewing the remains by relatives and friends, and a funeral oration by Col. Ingersoll. A large number of distinguished gentlemen were present. Soon after Mr. Ingersoll began to read his eloquent characterization of the dead, his eyes filled with tears. He tried to hide them behind his eye-glasses, but he could not do it, and finally he bowed his head upon the dead man's coffin in uncontrollable grief. It was after

some delay and the greatest efforts at self-mastery, that
Col. Ingersoll was able to finish reading his address, which
was as follows:

My Friends: 1 am going to do that which the dead often
promised he would do for me. The loved and loving
brother, husband, father, friend, died where manhood's
morning almost touches noon, and while the shadows still
were falling towards the West. He had not passed on
life's highway the stone that marks the highest point, but
being weary for a moment he laid down by the wayside,
and, using his burden for a pillow, fell into that dreamless
sleep that kisses down his eyelids still. While yet in love
with life and raptured with the world, he passed to silence
and pathetic dust. Yet, after all, it may be best, just in
the happiest, sunniest hour of all the voyage, while eager
winds are kissing every sail, to dash against the unseen
rock, and in an instant hear the billows roar a sunken ship.
For, whether in mid-sea or among the breakers of the far-
ther shore, a wreck must mark at last the end of each and
all. And every life, no matter if its every hour is rich
with love and every moment jeweled with a joy, will, at
its close, become a tragedy, as sad, and deep, and dark
as can be woven of the warp and woof of mystery and
death. This brave and tender man in every storm of
life was oak and rock, but in the sunshine he was vine and
flower. He was the friend of all heroic souls. He climbed
the heights and left all superstitions far below, while on
his forehead fell the golden dawning of a grander day.
He loved the beautiful, and was with color, form and music touched to tears. He sided with the weak, and with
a willing hand gave alms; with loyal heart and with the
purest hand he faithfully discharged all public trusts. He
was a worshipper of liberty and a friend of the oppressed.
A thousand times I have heard him quote the words:

"For justice all place a temple and all season summer." He believed that happiness was the only good, reason the only torch, justice the only worshipper, humanity the only religion, and love the priest.

He added to the sum of human joy, and were every one for whom he did some loving service to bring a blossom to his grave he would sleep to-night beneath a wilderness of flowers. Life is a narrow vale between the cold and barren peaks of two eternities. We strive in vain to look beyond the heights. We cry aloud, and the only answer is the echo of our wailing cry. From the voiceless lips of the unreplying dead there comes no word; but in the night of death hope sees a star and listening love can hear the rustle of a wing. He who sleeps here, when dying, mistaking the approach of death for the return of health, whispered with his latest breath, "I am better now." Let us believe, in spite of doubts and dogmas and tears and fears that these dear words are true of all the countless dead. And now, to you who have been chosen from among the many men he loved to do the last sad office for the dead, we give his sacred dust. Speech cannot contain our love. There was—there is—no gentler, stronger, manlier man.

NEW ❦ POPULAR BOOKS

PUBLISHED BY

RHODES & McCLURE,

CHICAGO.